"STOP STALLING, GARRET."

She could tell he wasn't used to being addressed with such fervor, yet she continued. "You're not telling the truth."

His eyes narrowed into a threatening stare. "I told you all I'm going to tell you right now. We'll talk about it when I get back."

"We'll talk about it right now," she insisted, leaning against the door. "Whether or not you want to admit it, Sarazen is my horse. I'm going to get him, and there's no way you can talk me out of it."

"Don't press me, lady," he said, pushing her aside. "He's your horse when I turn him over to you, and not a moment before."

Dear Reader,

Although our culture is always changing, the desire to love and be loved is a constant in every woman's heart. Silhouette Romances reflect that desire, sweeping you away with books that will make you laugh and cry, poignant stories that will move you time and time again.

This summer we're featuring Romances with a playful twist. Remember those fun-loving heroines who always manage to get themselves into tricky predicaments? You'll enjoy reading about their escapades in Silhouette Romances by Brittany Young, Debbie Macomber, Annette Broadrick and Rita Rainville.

We're also publishing Romances by many of your all-time favorites such as Ginna Gray, Dixie Browning, Laurie Paige and Joan Hohl. Your overwhelming reaction to these authors has served as a touchstone for us, and we're pleased to bring you more books with Silhouette's distinctive medley of charm, wit and—above all—*romance*. I hope you enjoy this book, and the many stories to come.

Sincerely,

Rosalind Noonan
Editor
SILHOUETTE BOOKS

MAXINE McMILLAN
Race for the Roses

Silhouette Romance

Published by Silhouette Books New York

America's Publisher of Contemporary Romance

SILHOUETTE BOOKS
300 E. 42nd St., New York, N.Y. 10017

Copyright © 1985 by Maxine McMillan

Distributed by Pocket Books

ISBN: 0-373-08378-5

First Silhouette Books printing August, 1985

10 9 8 7 6 5 4 3 2 1

America's Publisher of Contemporary Romance

Printed in the U.S.A.

MAXINE MCMILLAN
is so in love with horses that she couldn't help but include them in her first Silhouette Romance. She currently lives on the West Coast, and spends most of her time working to become a first-rate writer.

LONG ISLAND and environs

Chapter One

Adrianna Adams raised her binoculars and watched intently as the horses rounded the last turn and headed into the final stretch. Sarazen, the black stallion with the white diamond on his forehead, was too far on the outside to make up much ground from his fifth-place position. *He was poorly ridden,* she thought. *Right from the gate he was poorly ridden.* At the finish he was still gallantly making up ground, which said a lot for his noble heart. She wasn't sorry she made her uncle put the claim in for Sarazen on her behalf. Not sorry at all. He was a descendant of champions. How such a horse ever got placed into this cheap claiming race, she couldn't begin to imagine. But there he was. And her uncle, as an owner with a horse in the same race, was allowed to claim him for a ridiculously low price—six thousand dollars.

"Never buy a horse on impulse," her uncle Alex had warned her before the start of the race. "Everyone knows that. That horse never won a race in his life. If I put a claim in for him, I'll be the laughingstock of the track."

"Uncle, please. The race goes off in less than ten minutes!"

"All right, my dear. I can only hope, for your sake as well as mine, that someone else claims him and you lose him in the draw."

"I love you, Uncle Alex."

"You always say that whenever you get me to do something impulsive for you."

Impulsive? she thought. Just how impulsive was it to act on the opportunity she had been waiting for since she was ten years old? A chance to fashion out, from her love for horses, a lucrative thoroughbred-breeding business. She had known Sarazen would be running today and that her uncle's horse, Star Chase, would be in the same race. She had been planning to call him and invite herself to New York City to the races in the hope that she could get him to put in the claim for the black Arabian stallion. When he called to invite her to the track, it was more than mere coincidence. It was fate! Sarazen would be a great start.

Breeding horses was a gamble, but a promising one with the odds in favor of those who knew their horses. Adrianna knew as much about horses as anyone could know who had studied them for fourteen years. From the very first moment she saw her father leading her birthday present, the roan mare Flink, from the barn, she felt that something inside her had changed forever. She couldn't explain it, nor could anyone else. Horses became a part of her life. Through the years they dominated more and more of her interests and free time. Now, at the age of twenty-four, she couldn't imagine her life without them. *I will breed thoroughbreds,* she promised herself again and again. Not only was it something she had always wanted to do, but also it was a chance, maybe the only chance she had, to get her father out of debt. But she would have to be smart. And she would have to be careful. And she would have to leap quickly when the window of opportunity opened for her. Sarazen was that window. She knew it. She had to have him.

The entire track was bathed in the bright afternoon sun of the unusually warm spring day. The crowd, dressed in the colors of summer, seemed festive and alive, responding to the delightful weather with summer whites and cheery pastels. The smell of boiled hot dogs and mustard wafted up into the cool shade of the clubhouse level, a smell that Adrianna always associated with being in a crowd, in the open air in New York. And the sound was always the same—a static burbling, electric and tense, readying itself to roar when a field of horses galloped past towards the finish line.

The last time she was at Belmont Park Race Track was a year ago, just her and her uncle Alex. She had six winners that day. Alex called it beginner's luck. What a day that was! But today, hoping to buy a horse with her entire life's savings, she would need more than beginner's luck. Deep in thought, her eyes wandered over the crowd. A man standing in the adjacent aisle, down a few rows, caught her attention. He was wearing sunglasses. She couldn't see his eyes, but she felt he was looking at her. When she looked back a moment or two later, he was still there, watching. *Perhaps he thinks he knows me,* she thought, feeling self-conscious for even thinking he was looking at her. He was just too far away for her to be sure. When her uncle returned, she looked again. He had disappeared, sat down somewhere she hadn't noticed.

"I hope you didn't bet on Sarazen," her uncle said, lowering his large frame into the seat next to hers. "Buying him is one thing. Betting on him is something else. Even Star Chase beat him out. Here's your claiming receipt."

"Thanks, Uncle Alex." She took the receipt, and with it came a sudden surge of apprehension that she might have done a foolish thing.

"I pray someone else has claimed him," he said, opening his racing form in his lap. "Though for what, I can't imagine. Coming in fifth in that race was tantamount to a one-way ride to the glue factory."

He was exaggerating, she knew. Alex had the instincts of the consummate horse trader. He would never let on what it was he knew, nor would he admit he had ever made a mistake. Those were the rules of the game as he saw them, and they had served him well over the years. He had his own stable of over forty horses, and although he complained continually about how unlucky he was, Adrianna had never seen him without a limo at his beck and call, a live-in valet, and a cover-girl escort adorning his arm on his way to the grand opening of another celebrity watering-hole on posh Park Avenue. He was a fox, worldly-wise and shrewd, with years of experience behind him. His great weakness was his generosity to those he loved. He loved Adrianna and she knew it. If he chose to play his horse-trading game with her, it proved to her that she commanded a certain respect from him, and that meant more to her than never being able to trust a word he said.

"You're fooling no one, Uncle. Something tells me you're sorry you hadn't claimed Sarazen for yourself." *Was I bluffing,* she thought, *or was that wishful thinking to calm my nerves and settle the rumbling in my stomach?*

"Aha! You scamp!" He laughed. "Never trust a horseman, is that it? You've learned that rule well enough."

"I've had a master for a teacher," she replied.

"Flattery is my weakness. It will get you everywhere with me, and you know it. I didn't teach you a thing about horses you didn't already know. You're much too smart for me. Someday I'll get you to tell me where all that knowledge you have encased in that beautiful head of yours came from."

"Someday, Uncle, you'll stop trying to con me and speak the truth."

"Never!" He laughed, and the genuine good nature of the man sparkled in his eyes. He reached over and put his arm around her shoulder tenderly. "You're much too young and much too beautiful to get into this cutthroat business. I picture you in some gingham dress with wildflowers in your hair."

"Don't forget to add that my hands are folded, and my head is bowed, and I'm curtsying to every adult I'm presented to for their inspection. Right?"

"Something like that. I know I sound like an old fool, but I don't care. It's the prerogative of old age."

"You're not old, and you're not a fool." She touched his nose with the tip of her finger. "And quit trying to con me."

"I'll try," he said with a smile. "That's the best I can do. There's a horse trader behind those large brown eyes of yours. You know something you're not saying, and that's good. Trust nothing but your own instincts. And even then, don't even trust them!" He sat back to look at his racing form. "One bit of advice. Sarazen is owned by the Worthington stables. It's not like them to give up a horse that's worth anything. If you do get Sarazen, you might wish to have him carefully inspected before letting go of your hard-earned cash. He may indeed be the pig in the poke everyone thinks he is. Or has been led to believe he is. Be careful!"

She looked deeply into his face and saw the genuine concern he had for her. "I'm hearing the voice of experience talking, Uncle. I feel so . . . so innocent around you." She did.

"Now who is conning whom?" he teased. "Go get your horse. Good luck. Stable him in my stalls, if you wish. Before you go, who do you like in this race?"

"I'm not saying," she said, standing up. "But I'd stay away from the favorite if I were you."

"Scamp!"

"See you later. Which way to the office?"

No sense torturing herself. There was no way to know for sure if she had made the right choice. Her instincts told her that Sarazen was the opportunity she had been waiting for. But what assurance was that? Had she ever tested her instincts? Ever put up a small fortune because she just knew she was right? *Nothing ventured, nothing gained,* she thought as she presented her ticket to the steward in the track office. No one else had put in a claim for Sarazen.

"He's all mine?" She was elated and at the same time frightened. She had passed a point of no return. She had gone too far to back out now.

"If you're A. Trent, owner of Star Chase," he said, scrutinizing the demure feminine figure before him. She brushed her blond hair from her eyes and tried to calm herself for the sake of this business operation.

"He's my uncle," she explained.

"Your uncle, then, has the claim for Sarazen," he said perfunctorily. "Worthington Stables, three-year-

old stallion, black, white diamond marking on forehead, white cannons . . . ."

"No. The cannons are black," she corrected him.
The part of the leg from the knee to the hoof, the
shin, was black. "The pasterns, just above the hooves,
are white. The pasterns. No white cannons."

He ignored her comments and held out some forms.
"Have your uncle sign and return these papers here,"
he said, dismissing her.

"Is that all?" she asked, not taking the papers. She
sensed he was irritable because he thought he was
dealing with a mere child. She couldn't help how
young she looked; nor did she feel she had to apologize for it.

"Is there anything else?" he asked, impatient to be
rid of her.

"Why, no sir," she said sarcastically. "I'll get these
papers to my uncle right away," she said sweetly,
batting her eyelashes and pulling out her skirt to
curtsy. If he noticed the sarcasm, he paid no attention
to it.

She snatched the papers, and as she turned to leave
she saw that she was being watched by a tall, well-
dressed gentleman in a blue blazer. The smile on his
lips implied that he had seen her little act for the
steward and had found it amusing. He had the same
raven-black curly hair and was wearing the same light-
blue silk shirt as the man . . . he was the same man
she had noticed in the clubhouse grandstand. The
same man who had noticed her.

He held his sunglasses in his hand, and as she
watched him approach she thought, *why would anyone with such sparkling blue eyes as his ever wish to
conceal them? Eyes like diamonds.* She felt the power
of his penetrating gaze holding her transfixed and
captive. He was taller than she remembered, and

when he stood before her she had the most difficult time concentrating on what he was saying. Not that handsome a face, but a distracting and interesting one, if one were to study the parts separately. The nose was slightly crooked, broken perhaps, maybe more than once. The features were strikingly pronounced and well defined, ruggedly masculine, yet softened by a broad and generous smile. She wanted to examine him closely, but her face began to redden. Had he said something that made her blush? She didn't know. She hadn't heard a word he said.

"What did you say?" she asked.

"No need to get defensive," he said. The warmth of his smile vanished into the cold, menacing chill of his eyes. "Just horse talk. Or aren't you allowed to talk to strangers?"

"I allow myself to talk to whomever I wish," she said, piqued at yet another inference that she looked like a child. "You have some inside dope on the next race that you just have to tell someone about?"

She couldn't resist that crack, implying that he was a two-bit tout, a racetrack low-life who passes on tips on all the horses in a race to a number of unsuspecting suckers and then goes back to collect a reward for the information from whomever the winners happen to be. She knew he wasn't a tout. He was too expensively dressed.

"I have no inside information," he said. The insult had registered, but it brought back that pleasing smile of his. "Though, watching you go to the cashier's window as often as you do, one would think that you had all the information."

Watching her? How long had he been watching her? That knowledge made her feel uneasy, though she cautioned herself not to show it.

"I'm lucky, that's all," she said. "You need some luck for the next race?" She wanted to be sarcastic, but it didn't come out that way. Something inside her was pleased to know that he had been watching her. And for one unguarded moment, she entertained the thought that he may have found her attractive.

"I don't believe in luck," he said. "Besides, it's too late. The race just went off. Let's go outside and watch. Who did you bet on?"

He didn't wait for an answer, but touched her elbow and turned her towards the door. The strength in his fingers radiated throughout her body. When they reached the fence he released her, yet she could still sense the power in his grip. She tried to pretend to herself that she hadn't noticed the way his look had taken in her tweed jacket, the high collar of her pale pink blouse, and the pleated blue skirt that matched the color of his blazer perfectly.

She scrutinized him as he focused his binoculars on the track. "I didn't get a chance to bet," she said.

"Take a look." He offered her the glasses. The horses had already reached the quarter-mile turn, and the crowd, bunching at the rail, was beginning to stir with nervous expectancy. "Roam Away, the favorite, has a three-length lead. Would you have picked him?" he asked.

It was an innocent enough question. She liked the idea that this stranger would value her opinion. But his icy stare and a hint of amusement on his lips told her he was challenging her. And why she felt she had to accept the challenge, she couldn't imagine.

She snatched away his binoculars and trained them on the last turn leading into the stretch. The optical illusion was that of a multiheaded beast gliding atop a forest of hooves that pulverized the earth into a blizzard of dust and smoke. Here was where the positioning and the pacing of the first two-thirds of the race would pay off.

Dervish Dan was her pick, and he was now making his move as she knew he would have to. Stride for stride, staying half a length off Roam Away's flank, challenging for the lead. Could he overcome a natural tendency to just stay with the leading horse? Did he have the heart to win?

She lowered the glasses and offered him a challenge of her own. "Who do you like?"

He hesitated, studying her as if his pick were obvious. "If I were a betting man, I would pick . . . Roam Away."

Was that his pick, or an innuendo? She broke eye contact with him to watch the finish of the race. If he were a betting man, he wouldn't be playing the favorite. Not in this race, anyway.

"Even if Roam Away wins, he'll only pay ten cents on the dollar. Risking a dollar to make a dime seems like a foolhardy thing to do."

"I thought the idea was to pick the winner." His smile induced her to smile in return. He couldn't be more than thirty. *Maybe twenty-eight,* she thought. If he was trying to pick her up, he was doing an awful job of it. Though it was neat to tell someone how much she really knew about horses.

"The idea is not to lose," she said. "Dervish Dan is almost neck and neck with Roam Away already. He'll win by a nose. Even if he doesn't, he'll pay more for coming in second than the favorite will for winning. At six to one, the best bet is Dervish Dan to place. That's who I would have picked."

The din of the crowd boomed into a deafening crescendo, clamoring in the last few seconds of the race as Dervish Dan took the lead and nosed out

Roam Away for the win. She could sense that this exciting stranger was staring at her. She had to tell herself that she was not going to blush. She didn't.

"You seem to know a lot about racing." He slipped his binoculars into a leather case.

"Not as much as there is to know." It was a thrilling finish—no less exciting a race because she hadn't bet on it. Her heart was still pounding. Or was that because the race had ended and there was no longer any excuse to talk with this stranger? He was better-looking than she'd first thought. She liked the way he leaned against the fence and cocked his head towards her.

"You come to the track often?" he asked.

"As often as I'm in New York City. I love it! It's all very exciting, don't you think?"

"You don't live here, then?"

"No. I'm a country girl from way upstate." She could have bitten her tongue for saying that. No sense broadcasting that she wasn't the metropolitan sophisticate she tried to portray.

"Just a little ole country girl coming to the big city to make her fortune?" His tone seemed suspicious.

"If you wish." Her anger was mixed with regret that their conversation had to end on such a lousy note. "It was nice talking to you—until now. I should be getting back. Good-bye."

"Getting back to what? Your sugar daddy?" His eyes were ablaze, his face stiff with a fierceness that sent shudders down her spine.

"Sugar daddy? How dare you!" she gasped. "Just who do you think you are? What right do you have to—"

He stepped quickly in front of her and grabbed her arms. "None. No right at all. I'm sorry. Don't go. Please."

He held her so tightly she couldn't think of trying to move. "Let me go!"

As he released her, his troubled eyes scanned her face, searching for the correct thing to say. "Forgive me. I had no right to say that."

"You certainly didn't."

"Well, at least we're even now."

"Even? What on earth do you mean?"

"For that racing-tout crack. Do I really look like a racing tout to you?"

"Do I look like someone's . . . someone's . . . mistress to you?"

A smile brightened his face, chasing the clouds from his sky blue eyes.

"We're not getting off to a very good start, are we?" he said.

"No, we're not. Not that this . . . should continue any further than it has already." If she was to end this conversation, here was as good a place as any.

"It hasn't gone anywhere yet. You don't even know my name. What's yours?"

"Adrianna. And if you must know, that 'sugar daddy' I'm with is my uncle."

"Every mistress as young as you appear to be, out with a gentleman as old as he appears to be, insists for appearance's sake that she is with her uncle."

"I am his niece," she insisted, annoyed that he had her on the defensive once again.

"I know."

"You know? How do you know?"

"Instinct."

"Do you always trust your instincts?" He leaned against the fence and crossed his legs at the ankles. His gray slacks hugged his legs, revealing long and well-defined thigh muscles.

"When it comes to women and horses, I do."

Women and horses? What a chauvinistic conceit. "Well, your instincts may have failed you," she said. "You picked the wrong horse in that race, and you may just have picked up the wrong impression about me. I may very well be that gentleman's mistress, for all you know."

He studied her a moment, brazenly sweeping his eyes over her. "When an older gentleman indulges his ego, his escorts are invariably raving beauties with nothing more going on between their ears than a painted smile and a fluffy hairdo."

"How utterly charming. It's nice to know I'm not pretty enough to be mistaken for a mistress."

"You're not vacant enough." He took a step towards her and put his hands into the pockets of his slacks.

"I suppose that's a compliment."

"I don't know if it is or it isn't."

"You mean you don't care."

"Care to what—compliment you?"

Such self-confidence must be the source of his pride, Adrianna thought. *This man is used to having things his own way.*

"No. Care one way or the other what you say, or to whom. You're rude and you're insolent."

"No, I'm not." He smiled so innocently it totally disarmed her. "I'm just direct. Most people mistake that for rudeness. It isn't."

"You sure fooled me." Here was another good spot to say good-bye, but she needed the words, the correct words. It would be much simpler to just storm off.

"This has been one difficult encounter," he said, offering her his hand. "My name is Garret, and yours is Adrianna. Let's fast-forward this to the business at hand, shall we? If that's too direct, we can spar around awhile longer if it'll make you feel more at ease." She wanted to take his hand and shake on it, but what on earth would she be agreeing to? What business at hand? He saw her flinch as she overcame the impulse to touch his hand.

"Very well," he said, putting his hand back in his pocket. "It's a lovely day to be at the track, you look marvelous in that suit, let's see . . ." He looked at the sky, searching for something else to say. "I'm finding it very hard keeping my eyes off of you, where did you learn so much about racing, and why, in heaven's name, did your—uncle—claim Sarazen?"

"He didn't claim Sarazen. I did."

"Please. Your . . . Alex Trent claimed the horse, and I want to know why."

"He did it for me. I asked him to, not that it's any of your business. And you were going to say 'your sugar daddy,' weren't you? Not too sure if I'm his mistress or not? Instincts running out on you?"

There. The ball was in his court for a change, though the idea of her playing the femme fatale was ridiculous. She wouldn't know how to stand or how to pose.

"You want Sarazen because you think he's the most beautiful horse you've ever seen? And you just have to have him, is that it?"

"He's the most beautiful horse I've ever seen, but that's not the reason I want him."

"What is the reason?"

He certainly asked a lot of questions. From the apprehension she saw in his face, she suspected that this was the sole reason he'd had for talking to her.

"Has anyone ever told you you're too direct?" she said, no longer caring if she seemed the vamp or the country girl.

"Everyone," he said.

"Good. Then you should understand this. It's none of your business." It was the opportunity she had been waiting for. She turned to leave, but he placed a hand on her shoulder and gently turned her back around.

"You're right. It isn't. Let's have dinner."

"Are you asking me for a date?"

"In a subtle way. If I were being direct, I would have said 'your place or mine.'"

"How winsome. Tell me, what's the usual response you get with that . . . approach?"

"The usual response I get is 'my place,'" he said, biting his lip to keep from smiling.

"Of course. I should have guessed. Well, Garret, I already have a date, thank you."

"His place or yours?"

"His!" she said, coaxing the vamp back up onstage.

"Your uncle's?"

"My sugar daddy's. He's throwing this wonderful party at his estate. A lot of big shots and all. Sorry, some other time." That wasn't too bad, she thought, congratulating herself. Not quite what she had in mind, but one couldn't always dictate ideal circumstances. Well, what on earth was she supposed to say?

"I don't take no for an answer," he said.

"I'm charmed, but I didn't say no. I said some other time."

"Good. I'll see you at seven." The smile he had tried so hard to contain now filled his entire face.

"I didn't invite you! Besides, it's not my place to invite the guests."

"I can't wait to see you in something slinky and elegant," he said, with not even a pretense of concealing how enjoyable he found the thought.

"You don't know where he lives."

"Not to worry, I'll find it."

"I wasn't worrying."

"You were, but that's okay. I'll get there."

"You just can't come crashing in!" she said, knowing it was too late to say she didn't want him to come. She did. And he knew it.

"I want to see you tonight, and I will. That's pretty clear, isn't it?"

"Be prepared to be thrown out on your ear."

He touched her shoulders, and for one unguarded moment, she felt he was going to kiss her. He looked deeply into her eyes, turned and left her standing there. Watching him disappear, she thought he'd intended to prove that had he wanted to kiss her, there was nothing in the world she could have done to stop him.

Chapter Two

Her uncle's mansion on the north shore of Long Island was owned in the Prohibition days by a bootlegger who installed a small tower—a lookout—on the roof from which one had an unobstructed view of Long Island Sound. It was Adrianna's favorite spot in the entire house. From there, one could see across the Sound to Connecticut, or down onto the back veranda and lawn to count the guests at one of her uncle's innumerable parties and to scrutinize what the women were wearing. At Adrianna's sixteenth birthday party, her Aunt Frances had taken her up there to point out the people strewn about the lawn and had filled her ears with delicious anecdotes about each and every one of them: which children belonged to which adults, and which of the Barrington brothers was dating the striptease artist in New Jersey.

Though Frances had passed away the following year, Adrianna wished she were here with her now, in her bedroom, pointing out the window at the well-dressed people below, assigning them names, occupations, and untold secret adventures that only her aunt seemed to know anything about.

She hadn't been up to the lookout on this trip to New York. Too late to visit it now. Too dark to see anything but the lights on the faraway Connecticut shore.

Adrianna walked over to the floor-length mirror to inspect herself one last time. Her blond hair was meticulously styled to appear soft and casual. Her snug black velvet dress was cut from the shoulders into a sweeping plunge that revealed the swell of her breasts. She had never worn anything so elegant in her life. Just a single gold strand around her neck with one simple pearl decorated all this bare frontage. The slit running up the side of her leg exposed more of her thigh than she felt comfortable exposing. Too risqué? At least it was as far away from the homespun image of the young country girl as she could get.

She shut the lights off and walked back to the window to search through the throng of guests. No one even remotely resembled him. It was seven o'clock. She couldn't hide any longer. She could still feel the look he gave her just before he left that afternoon. Arrogant man. Insolent. It would be best not to think of him at all, and to put the thought of his crashing this party into proper perspective—as ridiculous and foolish. She had come to New York to get a horse; anything else was just a distraction. Downstairs, the guests were already nibbling hors d'oeuvres. She would head for the buffet and mingle.

When her uncle greeted her at the bottom of the stairs, the approval emanating from his admiring eyes didn't match his scolding tone. "You rascal! Where have you been? I was tempted to send out a search party for you."

"I was in my bedroom getting ready. Where was I supposed to be?"

"I forgot which bedroom you were in. In this house that could be fatal. You could have gotten locked in, and it would have been months before any of us were the wiser."

"Oh, Uncle!"

"Come," he said, offering his elbow, "we have to talk."

He escorted her through the foyer and past the living room, where she could only glimpse a few of the guests as they stood about in pockets of conversation, sipping champagne and munching finger food.

"The party looks divine. How many people have you invited?"

"Invited?" He stopped to wink at her. "I quit inviting years ago. That's something your Aunt Frances used to do. I just announce and hope for the best." He was wearing a black tuxedo with a large red rose pinned to his lapel. Adrianna thought that if he wore a sash across his chest, he would look like the perfect royal duke.

"Isn't that a bit dangerous?" she asked. "All kinds of people could come crashing in."

"That's half the fun. Let's see . . . you already know all the old fuddies. You should remember the neighbors—insufferable bores. I sometimes think they show up just to keep an eye on me. Frances must have made them promise to do just that."

"Not a bad idea." Adrianna smiled. "You need someone watching over you. Anyone who has as much fun as you do has got to be doing something deliciously evil."

"Never mind me. It's you I want to talk about." He pulled her into the library and closed the door. The room was extremely large, as all the downstairs rooms were. This was the only one distinctively masculine in decor. Heavy dark-oak paneling and shelving covered the walls, giving the room a somber, massive tone. The lounge chairs, grouped into clusters of twos and threes, were all covered in green leather stitched with brass studs. A hand-carved billiard table, lighted by a stained-glass Tiffany lamp, graced the center of the room.

"I might as well tell you now," he said. "This party is for you."

"Me? Uncle, what are you saying?"

"Inviting you to the races was just an excuse to get you to come to the city. There is someone here I want you to meet."

"I didn't come to New York to meet anyone." Garret's face flashed across her mind, jolting her in the pit of her stomach. How strange that a brief memory could have such a physical effect.

"I know. I know. The horse. Look, you're a beautiful young woman, and it's high time you started thinking about something else besides horses."

"You mean it's high time I got married?"

"Yes. But to the right man, of course."

"Of course. And you just happen to know who that man is?" Adrianna pulled away from him and walked over to the billiard table. "You have no right to interfere in my life. Not you, not my father, nor anyone else."

"I'm not interfering, Adrianna, believe me." He came up behind her and put his arm around her shoulder. "Listen to me. I just can't stand aside and watch you ruin your life with this crazy dream of yours. You need more than knowledge to make a go at this thoroughbred breeding business. You need luck. You need a handsome, well-bred, and thoroughly rich young man to—"

"To support me? And this craziness I have for horses could be just a hobby, a diversion to fill up the empty hours between the kids and the vacations?"

"You make it sound like a death sentence," he joked.

"Uncle Alex, I know your heart is in the right place, but you must believe me when I tell you I know what it is I want to do with my life. I'm not the naive little country bumpkin everyone thinks I am. I don't need anyone to take care of me."

"Maybe not," he said, lowering his voice and staring into her eyes, "but you're not fooling me. You'd do anything to get your father, my pigheaded brother-in-law, out of the clutches of the banks. Don't deny it. Throwing your life away after a dream is not the way to go about it. Besides, if he's too proud to take a loan from me, what makes you think he'll accept anything from you?"

Alex stood back to assess her reaction. He'd made a valid point. Her father was too proud to accept charity from anyone. His vineyard was a profitable operation at one time, before the blight destroyed over eighty percent of his crop. But it could be profitable again, just as soon as the new cuttings he'd imported from France started producing. It would take time. It would take someone like his daughter, the eventual inheritor of the business, to invest in it and keep it alive until it could flourish once again. A business investment. The only thing she could possibly talk her father into accepting. She would only be looking after her own interests. He would understand that.

"Let me worry about that, Uncle," she said, not wanting to explain anything further about herself or her father.

"Good. Worry about it. But in the meantime, what's the harm in just meeting this young man?"

"Uncle, I don't like the idea of your matchmaking for me!"

"I could have played dumb, you know. Just introduced him and let nature take its course."

"Yes, you could have. I wish you had."

"I've been doing that for years. And it's never worked," he joked.

"You are incorrigible!" she protested, but she couldn't stay mad at him for long.

"That's my girl. Now come along and be nice," he said, offering her his arm. "You get more beautiful every time I see you."

"But let me warn you, I'm not marrying anyone."

"Who said anything about marriage?"

"You did."

"Did I?"

"You're impossible, Uncle Alex."

"I know," he laughed.

It was an ordeal for Adrianna to meet Alex's neighbors again. They were wonderful people, but each of them had some remembrance of her when she was in braids and braces, climbing trees and roughhousing with the neighborhood kids. If she didn't know them better she would have sworn they were out to torture her.

The party was a sumptuous affair, as all of Alex's parties were. The fact that he had an ulterior motive in Adrianna's happiness was only an excuse. It was his annual spring bash, and she didn't have the heart to tell him that he would have given the party whether she was there or not. Someone at the piano in the corner was playing something familiar, and as Adrianna smiled at still another neighbor's reminiscence of how boyish she used to look, she hummed the tune silently to herself, hoping that whoever it was Alex was going to introduce her to would get there and rescue her from the conversation.

When Alex finally squeezed her hand as a signal and elbowed her into a small group of young men, she thanked him with her eyes for the promised relief.

"Jerald, I would very much like to present my niece, Adrianna."

Jerald was a good-looking young man with straight brown hair neatly combed off his forehead. She couldn't tell what color his eyes were, only that they seemed extraordinarily pleased to see her. She could only wonder at what Alex had told him about her. Maybe nothing. She offered her hand, and he touched it as gently as he would a teacup.

"Adrianna, this is Jerald Montgomery, of *the* Montgomerys. Don't let his wealth cloud your impression of him. He's a regular chap. Aren't you, Jerald?" Alex said, slapping him on the back.

"A regular chap, Mr. Trent," Jerald said, condescending to smile at Alex's camaraderie.

"Well, I'll leave you two alone. Jerald, introduce Adrianna to your friends, and I'll see what mischief I can stir up elsewhere." Alex winked at Adrianna before he turned away.

"You'll have to excuse him," she said of Alex as he left. "He's a pest of the first order."

"Not at all," Jerald said, bouncing on his toes as if he was at a loss for something to say. *He couldn't be much older than me,* Adrianna thought, watching him fumble his hands away into his pockets. *Perhaps younger. Oh, Uncle Alex, is this your grand young man?*

Jerald's friends were equally shy, heaving up their adoring smiles with nothing more to offer by way of conversation than a nod. One of them didn't even bother to turn around to acknowledge her.

"Oh, er, Adrianna," Jerald finally said, "this is Binky, and this is Jonathan—we call him Johnny—and this . . . gentleman, I don't believe I've had the pleasure."

The man who had his back to Adrianna turned and grabbed her hand.

"My name is Garret. Garret Malone," he said, riveting her motionless with his icy blue eyes. Garret! His sudden appearance took her breath away. He had said he would come, and there—here—he was. "There's dancing out on the veranda. It would be my pleasure if you would allow me the honor."

She couldn't say anything. The crystal chandelier behind him sparkled through the curls of his raven black hair, surrounding him with an aura of light. Adrianna trembled. It was as if suddenly, in this crowded room, they were entirely alone.

"If you'll excuse us, gentlemen," he said. Not waiting for their permission, he pulled her by the hand and led her through the crowd.

"How did you get in here?" she said, wresting her hand free when they got outside.

"Through the front door, like everyone else. Why?"

"I mean . . . why? Why are you here?"

"I told you this afternoon. I wanted to see you all dressed up. Elegant and slinky." He stepped back to get a better look at her and smiled. "I'm impressed. I didn't think you could look this good. Had I known you were going to all this trouble for me, I would have come a lot sooner."

"For you?" The soft lights of the veranda did nothing to soften his self-centeredness. "That's a bit presumptuous, don't you think?"

"Maybe. But you are glad to see me, so there is no sense denying it."

"Don't misread shock for joy, Mr. Malone. You're the last person on earth I expected to see. Do you know my . . . do you know Alex Trent well?"

"Not personally. And no, I wasn't invited."

"Don't look so pleased. Neither was anyone else."

He was wearing a tuxedo, and it made him look taller than she remembered. More handsome, too.

"No wonder I had no trouble getting in here." His smile was genuine and infectious, and if she didn't feel she had to be angry she would be smiling at him right now. "I was prepared, however."

He reached into the inside pocket of his jacket, pulled out a leather wallet and flipped it open. It was an ID identifying the bearer as a reporter for the *Royal Globe*, the national gossip magazine.

"Well, so that's who you are," Adrianna said. "It explains everything."

"I borrowed this from a friend. Noel Bauer. Look, his picture is on it." In the corner was a small picture that could be construed, in poor lighting, as a resemblance, but hardly anything more.

"Noel? I like that name. I like it better than Garret. So, you're Noel Bauer, the gossip columnist? I never would have guessed."

"It's better than any invitation. There isn't a host or hostess on the entire continent that wouldn't be thrilled with having a real gossip writer in their midst."

"Come now, Noel, you're too modest. Tell me,"

she said, stepping close to him to whisper, "what dirt have you dug up so far tonight?"

He was about to insist on his identity, but he thought better of it and placed the ID back into his pocket.

"The truth is out," he said, grabbing her arm and pulling her even closer to him. "It's imperative that you keep my secret. If anyone should know, well, they'll be so guarded and self-conscious, I'll never get anyone to open up with anything juicy and vulgar for my readers. Promise?"

"Your secret is safe with me," she said, marveling at his ease and willingness to play her game. *He's going to go along with it. And turn it to his advantage if I'm not careful. He is not going to get the better of me,* she thought, itching to knock off some of that smug self-confidence of his.

"Good. I knew I could count on you. Shall we dance?"

A small gazebo out on the lawn had been converted into a garden bandstand. A four-piece orchestra was playing a dreamy melody from the forties, and when he put his arm around her waist and lifted her a bit off the floor, she was unable to resist. The cool night air sharpened the smell of his cologne, a strong masculine scent that complemented the strength in his arms and the hardness of his legs as he pressed them so casually against hers.

"You know, you shouldn't be out here dancing," she said, noting to herself how expertly he led her around the floor. "All the action is inside. Mrs. Barrington—I'll introduce you—has anecdotes about everybody in the racing world. I don't know anything about anyone."

"I thought I would do a piece about horse racing. You know—owners, trainers, the stories behind the stables. That sort of thing," he said, checking the success of his ploy with a smile that challenged her to think of a comeback.

"Well, you've picked the wrong person. I just bought my first racehorse today. The only owner I know is Alex Trent. You would do much better talking to him."

"I think I'm doing quite well here."

The song ended and they stopped moving, but he didn't let her go. He held her as if the music would start again momentarily. She stood there, speechless, losing herself for the moment in the depths of his blue eyes.

"I'm sorry," he finally said, "did you say something?"

She hadn't said a thing. He still didn't let her go. She was beginning to wonder at the silly game she had started and just what it was that was so important for her to prove, so comfortable did she feel just standing there in his arms.

"I said . . . the music stopped," she lied.

"So it did." He let her go, and the night air chilled her shoulders, making her wish she was back in the warmth of his arms.

She spotted her uncle through the window, shuffling through the crowd towards the veranda.

"Here comes Alex," she said. "I'll bet he's disappointed that I'm not with . . . Jerald Montgomery."

"Of *the* Montgomerys," he said. "I overheard him introducing you."

"I suppose I should know who *the* Montgomerys are," she said, "but honestly, I haven't a clue. Do you?"

"No. And I don't care to find out."

"A fine gossip columnist you are. They may very well be the rage."

"I don't care to know about anyone at this party except you. Let's go for a walk. Show me around this estate."

"Not a chance," she said. "I know less about you than I do about Jerald. I'm not giving you the opportunity of cornering me in some dark recess."

"So, you do have designs on me. I'm flattered," he said, stepping back and putting his hands on his hips.

"Of all the conceited . . . I'll have my uncle toss you out of here!"

"Your uncle?" He laughed. "I thought he was your sugar daddy. You certainly look pretty enough now to be anyone's mistress."

"Adrianna?" Alex called from the doorway. "Where's Jerald?"

"Is that a question or an accusation, dear Uncle?" she said, holding her temper, deciding on how best to end this little charade once and for all. "Come over here and meet Mr. . . . . Bauer!"

Garret looked surprised, but only for a moment. Before turning to greet her uncle, he gave her a playful wink that said she would have to do better than that.

"Noel Bauer, sir," Garret said, extending his hand. "From the *Royal Globe*. Forgive me for not announcing myself sooner. My paper is doing a story on the most beautiful estates on Long Island, and I've picked yours to be featured in next month's issue. Your niece has graciously offered to show me around and fill me in on some of the history associated with the house. I'm sorry I've taken up so much of your time, Miss Adams."

Was he going to leave?

"You're a reporter, and you want to do a history of the house?" Alex asked, suddenly ignited with enthusiasm. "What a great idea! This place has more stories than a medieval castle. It was owned by racketeers in the Prohibition days."

"Uncle, please . . ."

"It's true. They even built a lookout on the roof. They smuggled in booze from Canada. Why, it's been rumored that every bottle of scotch entering this country in 1928 was carried off my dock down at the beach."

"How interesting," Garret said, again winking at Adrianna. Was he asking her to play along, or was he surprised that his ploy had suddenly grown unmanageable? "A lookout on the roof? I would very much like to see that. Perhaps some other time. I don't wish to interfere with your party."

"Nonsense. Nonsense. I'd take you up there myself, but Adrianna has played up there as a child. She'd be glad to show it to you, won't you, my dear?"

"Uncle, this has gone far—"

Garret grabbed her hand and held it in both of his. "It would be my honor," he said. "I couldn't thank you enough."

"I have a hundred stories I could tell you," Alex said, grinning like a Cheshire cat as he thought through the possibilities. "Adrianna, show him around. And when you're through, we'll talk in the library. I have a story that'll curl your socks, young fella!"

"But, Uncle! What about . . . Jerald?"

"Jerald? Oh, Jerald. I'll keep him entertained until you get back. Be careful up there. Those wooden stairs aren't as trustworthy as they once were."

Alex stepped back into the party as if rejuvenated by a sudden stroke of good fortune and in a moment disappeared among the guests.

"I'm sorry," Garret said, reaching out to touch her shoulder. "Seems to be a decent guy. I didn't enjoy leading him on. I had no idea he'd grab onto it like that. I'll apologize to him and set it straight." Something within her knew he was telling the truth.

"You'll break his heart. I'll bet he's bragging right now to his envious neighbors. Whom I hope you are ready for. They'll be streaming out here after you like the hounds after the fox."

"Do you think so?"

"I know so, and I can't wait. It'll be such fun watching you double-talk your way past people who actually read the gossip magazines."

"You'd enjoy that, wouldn't you?" He smiled.

"Immensely."

"You'll just have to rescue me, then."

"Oh?"

"You wouldn't want them to find out I'm an imposter, and that your uncle had been made a fool of, would you?"

Was there no way to top this man? "I'd like very much to see that tower," he went on. *"Now,* if you don't mind, while we can still make our getaway."

His expression was serious and almost matter-of-fact, as if the only option she had left had been carefully thought through and mutually agreed upon. *How did this happen?* she wondered as she turned to lead him off the veranda and onto the pathway along the side of the house. She should have been furious at him, but she wasn't. He had outwitted her. His presence, once so threatening, was suddenly reassuring in the darkened shadows of the house.

"Here's the staircase. Three flights up and you're there. It's a clear night. You should be able to see Stamford." Without warning, he reached down and picked her up into his arms. "What do you think you are doing?!"

"With that tight dress and high heels, you'd never make it to the top. Relax. I won't drop you."

"I am perfectly capable of walking. And if you don't agree, you can just leave me here and go up yourself."

"And waste that beautiful view of Connecticut with no one to share it with?" He held her effortlessly. As he mounted the stairs, she let her head drop back, so that it was dangerously close to his lips. She could feel his breath against her cheek.

"Watch the road," she said when he looked too deeply into her eyes.

"Afraid?"

"Terrified," she lied.

"I won't let you go."

"That's not what I'm terrified of."

He stopped a step or two before the last landing. The bone-white light of the moon gleamed softly in his eyes. A quiet breeze whispering through his curly hair chased away the warmth of his breath, making her shudder involuntarily in the cool night air.

"Are you cold?"

She wasn't. "I'm freezing," she lied.

He carried her onto the platform and slowly released her. Her toes barely touched the floor, he held her so tightly with one arm around her waist. He slipped his other warm hand around her shoulders, protecting her from the night air.

The tower was small and circular, open on all sides above a four-foot wall and railing. The roof, shaped like a cone to match the Victorian peaks of the mansion, cast a shadow in the moonlight that blocked out his face.

"There's Stamford, over there," she said, feeling an apprehension that the shadow now masking his face would suddenly make him lose his inhibitions.

"So beautiful," he said, but he hadn't turned to take in the view. His nose touched her forehead. He was talking about her.

"Garret . . . ." Her hands were behind his neck, her fingers dangerously close to tangling themselves in his luscious hair. "This is . . . I don't even know who you are."

"How could you? We just met today."

"How brilliant. Why didn't I think of that?"

"What is it you want to know?"

His hands slid down to her waist, and he lifted her up so that her nose was now touching his. What was it that she had to know?

Music from the little orchestra in the garden meandered its way up to the roof, mixing into the breeze, into the lights on the faraway shore, into the sudden stillness of her heart that stopped her breath when she knew they were going to kiss.

Chapter Three

He didn't kiss her. When she opened her eyes she found him studying her, glancing over her features one by one as if he were committing them to memory. She felt more foolish than annoyed. Why didn't he kiss her when he had the chance, she wondered, imagining the sensation of his lips pressed against hers.

His hands, still firm around her waist, lifted her higher till her nose was but an inch above his. He kissed her cheek along the edge of her jawbone, sending an electrifying chill down the center of her back. Pleasure or pain? She wasn't sure. She only knew that suddenly it was impossible for her not to respond. Unwittingly, she leaned back and pulled his face into her soft flesh.

His teeth nibbled at her earlobe, and his breath on her bare shoulders excited a sense of vulnerability in her. How totally helpless she was, being held in the hands of this man. A shudder quaked slowly through her, intensifying the pleasure that groaned in her throat, frightening her but at the same time holding her still, waiting for more. His lips tantalizingly caressed the skin along her plunging neckline. The intoxicating warmth of his mouth was awakening sensations she never knew existed. Why couldn't he just kiss her?

Adrianna had to protest, to push him away, even though she craved his kiss more than she had any man's in her entire life. She placed her hands against his shoulders, but they quickly betrayed her, escaping into the luscious shocks of his hair as if mindless of the fear inside her. The scent from his hair was heady and intoxicating. How could something so masculine smell so warm and inviting?

She would have to discourage him while there was still time—free herself, if only for a moment.

"Garret, please . . . ." Her arms, suddenly empty, ached to wrap themselves around him once again, but she forced her hands to push his shoulders away.

He let her down slowly. His face seemed so gentle, almost dreamy, in the shadows that softened his features and fashioned out of the darkness another stranger, more mysterious and exciting than the one before. Those strong limbs that held her so easily now closed around her body, pulling her up against him. His lips found hers and playfully began to stir a delicious miracle of sensations she had never dreamed about.

She was losing her self-control. It was impossible not to savor the excruciating thrill his virility elicited from her. A new and dangerous receptiveness ached deep inside her, threatening to shatter her control.

He pulled his head away, and she could see the passion in his eyes. He whispered something, but all she heard was a moan, a warning that he was no longer teasing. His mouth found hers open and willing. As they plunged into another kiss, his hands slid down her back, pulling her against him again. The intensity of his passion sent trembles of emotion through her legs, her thighs. His hand slowly and firmly found her breast, and the touch shocked the breath from her. She broke the kiss.

"Stop . . . please stop."

They were up against the railing, out of the shadows of the roof. His face, iced white by the full light of the moon, only stiffened in resolve. His urgency was frightening.

She clutched his hand in both of hers, and he permitted her to move it. Like iron in velvet, she thought. At any moment he could turn his strength on her and take what he thought he was invited to take. She had responded to him. She couldn't deny that, nor would she even try. No man had ever excited her more.

"I know you must have had many women . . . respond to your advances. . . ." She bit the inside of her lip, going over what she wanted to say, hoping she wouldn't falter and betray in words what her body had already confirmed. "But . . . not this time."

"You've made up your mind, then?" he said. His smile was knowing and triumphant, as if he had expected her to resist.

"Yes, I have. I—"

"There's no need to explain," he said, taking his hand from hers and reaching for her waist. "Sit up here." He lifted her up to the railing, and she leaned against one of the pillars supporting the roof. Her black velvet dress and his black tuxedo disappeared in the darkness. Her arm resting on his shoulder seemed, for a moment, suspended in space. "You're more beautiful than I imagined you could be."

That simple statement troubled him, as if suddenly the rules had changed and he didn't like having to adjust to a new game. His fingers caressed her cheek and then lifted her chin. Was it the moon, or the lights across Long Island Sound, or the stars sprinkled on the velvet sky that ignited the longing within her?

"Now, before I kiss you again, ask me some questions so that we'll no longer be total strangers."

"Let's see. Who are you? What do you do? Where do you live?"

"Hold on. Just one thing at a time. Something that doesn't need a lot of explanation. I find it very difficult to stay away from you. One question, one kiss. Agreed?"

What kind of game is this? she wondered, feeling the little girl inside her charmed by the idea of it. She had a thousand questions. If she had to pay for every one of them with a kiss . . . ? There was just too much to know about him. The idea was silly, childish. No, she would not agree to play his game. She tried to gather her breath and dismiss the effect the aroma of his skin was having on her. Why did she feel compelled to touch his face, to outline his lips with the tip of her finger?

"Why . . . why did you come here tonight?" She knew the answer to that already. To see her. "No. What I meant to say was, where . . . ?"

"Where was I born?" he suggested.

What difference did it make where he was born? At one kiss per question she had to be more selective, get as much information from him as she could before it was no longer necessary to know anything about him. Before the only thing that really mattered was how well her body could withstand the hunger in his eyes.

"New York City."

He leaned forward and took his kiss, a soft and open graze of his lips on hers. No rush. No urgency this time. Just a gentle flutter across her lips.

"When?"

Why did she ask that?

"Twenty-eight years ago."

Again a simple touch of his lips. Simple and easy. Well under control. A fingertip had curled itself into a lock of his hair, but it was easily untangled. She broke the kiss.

"Do you like living in New York?"

Was she going insane? What did it matter if he liked or disliked living in New York? Another wasted question she'd have to pay for.

"I'm happy wherever I live."

The stubble on his chin rasped with a tingling feeling as it brushed against her cheek. He kissed the pocket of her neck between her earlobe and jaw. The sensation sent a chill racing down the side of her body, making her squirm. Did she dare ask another question? *Maybe just one more,* she thought. He pulled away and watched her as she tried to think.

"I can't hear you," he whispered, kissing her lightly on the nose.

"How many . . . ?"

"How many women have I had?" he asked, reading her mind. "Just one shy of the one I want."

He placed his large hands on her shoulders, and they made her think of how small she was in comparison to him. She never allowed herself to feel frail or weak with any man. She was raised by a stern and loving father, a widower who gave her the encouragement to live in a man's world and do whatever it was she set her mind and heart to do. She never had a stereotyped female role model to follow. The men she knew, mostly boys from college, were young and unsure of their masculinity. They needed frailty to bolster their images of themselves. They never got it from her. It was the reason no man she had ever met asked her out more than once. And no one had ever kissed her the way this . . . this stranger had. *He doesn't need weakness or frailty,* she thought, watching his eyes change color in the moonlight.

Hooking his thumbs under the straps of her dress, he slid them off her shoulders. His eyes became more and more wistful as they swept over her face and neck. "I can't play this game anymore," he said. "Either we talk, or we make love. And this is the only time I'll ever ask you to decide."

"We talk," she said, knowing he meant every word. It was the way he said it that irritated her. "Don't threaten me. Don't tell me what you are going to do with or without my permission."

"No threat," he said, lifting the straps of her dress back to her shoulders. "Just a simple statement of fact."

"That may charm your other lady friends, but it does nothing for me." His hands tightened on her arms, and as he pulled her close, the dauntless confidence in his eyes warned her to be cautious.

"Don't press your luck, lady. I'm not a toy you can play with."

"Neither am I," she said. Finally, he released her, turning to lean on the railing that looked out over the Sound towards Connecticut. It was the first time she could remember that he'd looked at anything but her.

She had come a long way these past few minutes, and part of her was grateful that she had come through unscathed. She watched him closely, studying the silhouette of his profile as she tried to remember how his face felt against her neck. Another few seconds and the impressions his body made on hers would be locked up in her memory. Who was this man to just barge his way into her life as though he had every right to be there?

"Where's Stamford?" he said, scanning the lights on the distant shore. He was trying to make conversation. The exhilaration of the last few minutes smoldered away inside her. How could she allow herself to be so manipulated?

"I don't know. It's over there somewhere," she said, not wanting to talk.

"Where? Point," he said.

"I don't know which one is Stamford. There." She pointed at a group of lights. "I think it's in that direction."

"No need to get angry." A smile creased his cheeks. She sensed he knew exactly how she felt and why, and that he knew there wasn't a thing she could do about it.

"I'm not angry," she lied. "There's Stamford. Now that you've seen it, it's time I was getting back to the party." She slid off the railing and straightened her dress.

"I thought you wanted to talk?"

"You thought wrong. Talk was the only real option you gave me. We talked. Now I'm ready to rejoin the party."

"Why? You would much rather be up here with me."

"Don't tell me where I would rather be."

"Someone has to. You're obviously not old enough to figure it out for yourself."

He stood in front of her, blocking her way to the stairs.

"I'm old enough to know that conceit and arrogance are the stock-in-trade of boorish egomaniacs. Good night, Mr. Malone, or whoever you are. Maybe we'll see each other at the racetrack sometime!"

She couldn't see his face clearly enough in the shadows to assess his reaction; she only saw that his hands were about to touch her shoulders to keep her from moving. He put them in his pockets instead.

"That's very good. I'm impressed. Now sit down and let's talk."

"I've had all the conversation I can take for one night, thank you. Now, if you'll just stand out of the way . . ." He didn't budge. ". . . or do I have to scream?"

"You'll have to scream. But before you do that, I'll have one last kiss. Then you can scream your fool head off."

"You love telling people what to do, don't you?"

"Some people need to be told."

"Well, just in case you haven't figured it out yet, I don't need to be told anything." He took a step closer and drew his hands from his pockets.

"You need to be told everything," he said. "You need to be told what it is your body is begging for but your mind is unable to admit." He pulled her hard up against him. His body was a wall of granite, immovable and powerful. "You need to be told how beautiful you are and that little girls shouldn't play big-girl games."

"I don't play games."

"You do. Only you're too innocent to know it. I'm

letting you off easy this time. Next time, you'll show more respect for the power you have packed into that cute little frame of yours." His voice went soft and gentle, and his hands found her waist and encircled it like an iron band. "Next time, you'll be more honest with yourself and with your feelings. You'll know exactly why you kiss me the way you do and why you want me to kiss you. You know it already but you can't admit it. I don't expect you to believe this—I'm having trouble admitting it myself—but from the very first moment I saw you, I . . ."

He lifted her up to his face, beckoning her to look in his eyes and see what he was unable to say.

She didn't know what it was he wanted her to see. She only found intensity and conviction, and that frightened her.

"Put me down. Please."

"Not until I get that kiss. And that, lady, is not a threat, it's a promise."

"I'll scream."

"You already said that."

She felt weightless, suspended in space before him. The lights and the stars behind him disappeared in the blur of her anger. She was trapped. She knew it was useless to resist. He would have his kiss, then, she decided, if that was the price she would have to pay for her freedom. But he would not enjoy it. He would not make demands that would go unchallenged, she promised herself. No man would ever have this advantage over her again, she told herself. It wasn't very likely she would meet anyone like him again. His strength alone was remarkable, not to mention the magnetism of his blue eyes. . . .

"Have your kiss, then," she said, pressing her closed lips against his and then pulling away.

"I said a kiss. From a woman. You haven't already forgotten how, have you?"

Forgotten? How could she forget the deep magic of their earlier kiss?

"I'll hold you here all night if I have to."

"You . . . you . . . there are women in the world who detest these strong-arm tactics. Maybe you've never met any of them before, but—"

"Just shut up and kiss me. Or are you going to force me to steal it from you?"

"Force you?" She folded her arms across her chest. "That'd be the day!"

He looked over her shoulder, found the railing, and sat her on it. "This is going to take longer than I thought," he said. His hands were on the rail to either side of her. He leaned closer, and she had to hold on to his neck to keep her balance. He kissed the edge of her cheekbone and nuzzled his nose into her ear. "Go on. Finish what you have to say."

"You're not listening to anything I'm saying."

"I'm listening." He nibbled at her earlobe and then kissed her neck, again in that spot just under her ear.

"Men think that women are responsible for their passions and are totally to blame if they can't, or won't, control their . . . natural urges."

"Natural urges?" he whispered. His breath tickled her neck, and she squirmed to avoid having to react. "I've never had trouble getting my natural urges satisfied."

"I bet you haven't."

"Are you finished talking, or is there something else you want to teach me about men and their . . . natural urges?"

"I wouldn't be that presumptuous."

"You would if I allowed it."

She closed her eyes and tried to swallow her rage.

"Have you had enough? I'd like to get back to the party now."

He said nothing, just kissed her neck gently as if he had all the time in the world. He was so frustratingly slow and so painstakingly deliberate. When his mouth finally reached hers, it was with a sense of relief that she responded to him, unable to deny the excitement his mouth breathed into hers. How could she resist as his lips touched hers with a warm, sensuous stroke that crystallized the tension in her jaw, tightened her chest and stopped her breath? She knew at once, with every fiber in her being, that if she moved, she would never be able to stop.

He pulled back far enough to see her face.

"You look like you've seen a ghost," he said.

A ghost? A good choice of words. There was a ghost inside her, threatening to flicker through her hands, locking them into his hair and pulling his face, those eyes, closer.

She regained her breath and the frightening spirit escaped through her nostrils, exhausting what strength she had left to resist him. He had awakened a new spirit within her, and she was terrified at the prospect. He had conjured up a demon inside her, a passion that gnawed away all of her self-conceptions, leaving an aching emptiness, a gaping space of pain and pleasure so deep within her.

"You can scream now," he said, backing away from her. She was too frightened to scream. She wanted to cry. "Go back to your party."

Just like that. Now that he had what he wanted, he was dismissing her. She slid off the railing. He reached for her arm to help her, but she pulled away from him and walked to the stairs.

"Thank you, Mr. Malone," she said as sarcastically as she could, "for allowing me to leave. I hope that you have gotten everything you came for." She watched him a moment, drinking in the image that she knew was going to haunt her for a long time to come. She hated him for showing her how vulnerable she was, how easily he could touch her, how completely in control he was.

"I always get what I want," he said, taking a step out of the moonlight and almost disappearing in the shadows. "Whatever I set my mind to."

"How nice. I wish I could say the same." She turned from the shadows and stepped out on the landing of the staircase. She could see a few couples strolling in the garden below.

"You can't get down those stairs in that dress and with those shoes." His voice sounded faraway, soft with solicitude, as soft as the shadows masking him.

The steps were steep and her dress was tight. She leaned against the railing to kick off her shoes.

"You'll just have to get down the same way you got up." He was next to her before she knew it, and in an instant she was off her feet and swept up into his arms. "The best way to carry you down would be to put you over my shoulder." He made a motion as if he was going to toss her over his shoulder like a sack of flour.

"Don't you dare!" she protested.

"Lady, you are beautiful. What's so startling about it is that you don't even know it."

"Just . . . get us down from here," she said, knowing it was useless to try to break free. Her heart was pounding his words into her ears. He descended slowly and carefully, stopping before he reached the last step.

"I'll see you tomorrow. We'll have dinner. We have a lot to talk about."

"Are you telling me? Or are you asking me?"

"I'm telling you. If I asked you, you'd say no. And then I'd have to think of something drastic, something that would undoubtedly get you all up in a huff."

"Why don't you try asking, for a change? Maybe I won't say no."

"Will you have dinner with me tomorrow?"

"No."

"See what I mean?" He took the last step and put her down.

"You're just ordering me around. Period. No. We will not have dinner tomorrow, or any other time. I'm going to pick up my horse tomorrow, and with any luck, I'll be well on my way home by tomorrow night. It was nice meeting you." She spun around and walked away.

"Okay. We'll play it your way," he called after her. She could detect a trace of merriment in his voice. "Seafood? French? Or Italian?"

She didn't dare stop or turn around. Say nothing . . . nothing . . . just keep walking. What an insufferable, arrogant, unbelievable man!

Her uncle was on the veranda with a few of his neighbors. She didn't want to talk to him or to anyone else. All she wanted to do was get into her bedroom, lock out the world, and begin the arduous process of getting that man out of her mind.

"Adrianna?" her uncle called out to her. "Where's that columnist? Did you show him the lookout? The Blanchards here think he'll love their Victorian, especially the secret room in the cellar."

She glanced behind her, knowing that he would be gone. "He had to run. You know how writers are. He had a deadline to meet."

"I wanted to show him more of the house before the Blanchards could drag him off to their place."

"Have you ever been in our cellar, Adrianna?" Mr. Blanchard asked. The Blanchard house was the third one along the shore, eastward from her uncle's.

"No, Mr. Blanchard. But if I see him again, I'll be sure to tell him about it."

"What is it, dear?" Alex asked, taking her by the arm and walking her to a quiet place on the veranda.

"Nothing. Why?"

"You look pale."

"Just a bit tired. I'd like to lie down for a while."

"Did that writer get fresh with you?" Uncle Alex's protective instincts were still very much alive, and she loved him for his concern.

"No, Uncle. Nothing like that. Only, you might as well know, he wasn't a writer. He had a phony credential with him in order to crash the party. I thought I was playing a joke on him by forcing him to play the part. I'm sorry, Uncle Alex, it was all my fault. He didn't mean to deceive you."

"Sorry? For what? No one enjoys a good joke better than me. You look as if that young man has something over on you."

"Hardly. I met him this afternoon at the track office when I was claiming Sarazen. I won't be seeing him again."

"That makes you sad," he said, putting a fatherly arm around her shoulder.

"Are you asking me, or are you telling me?"

He didn't answer, but kissed her on the forehead. "Come, the night is young. That millionaire I lined up for you has been poking about the place looking for you ever since you left. Did you like him?"

"Who?"

"Never mind. I can see by that look in your eyes that you had better go and lie down."

"What was his name again?"

"Who? Your young man?"

"The millionaire."

"Why?"

"What do you mean, why?"

"Why are you fooling yourself?" he said. "What I had hoped would happen between you and Jerald seems to have happened between you and that stranger."

"Oh, please. You're just too . . . romantic. Nothing happened between me and that . . . that stranger."

"Oh? Then tell me, where are your shoes?"

Chapter Four

No matter how hard she tried, Adrianna couldn't sleep. She welcomed the gray dawn as a reprieve from the torment of a restless, trouble-filled night. Maybe now, she thought, she could stop reliving those moments she'd spent with Garret, analyzing the endless messages in the nuances of his look, the meaning in the strength of his hands as they circled around her waist. Enough. It always ended the same way, with his face shadowed in moonlight just a breath away, poised for one eternal moment before . . .

She stood up, fighting off the tiredness from having stayed awake all night, and walked to the window. There were no clouds in sight. It would be another grand day.

The window opened into the room, and the cool morning rinsed the night air out of her, filling her with a sense of expectancy and promise. She had a lot of work to do today. Close the deal on Sarazen, arrange a trailer for his transport, and—she hoped—be on the road by nightfall with her horse in tow, one giant step closer to fulfilling her dream.

She showered quickly and dressed in western-style jeans, a checkered cowboy shirt, and ranch boots that hugged her calves as if they were made for her. They looked like fancy riding boots, but the leather was thick and worn soft by use and hundreds of applications of linseed oil and saddle soap.

She slipped a bandanna behind her neck and knotted her hair into a ponytail. At least the fatigue didn't show in her face, she thought as she carefully applied her makeup. Maybe her eyes were just a little glazed and troubled. But that wasn't fatigue. She forced herself to stop thinking of Garret. The sounds of china clinking on the veranda below reminded her that the empty feeling in her stomach was due mostly to a simple lack of food. She was ravenous.

A few servants were out on the grass, folding the lawn chairs and tidying up. As she leaned out the window, she thought she caught the aroma of coffee. There were people eating on the veranda, but she couldn't see them. Guests? Alex loved to have guests stay over after a party. It just provided him with another opportunity to lavish his generosity upon them and extract from them the companionship he seemed to need more and more as he grew older.

On her way to the veranda, she stopped off in the kitchen and poured herself a cup of coffee. Marcie, the cook—a permanent fixture after countless years of service to the Adams household—was busy at the stove, barking orders over her shoulder at the kitchen help as they arranged plates and trays on the serving carts for her inspection.

"Adrianna?" she called out, wiping her hands on her apron. "What are you going to have for breakfast? And don't tell me just a strip of bacon and a roll. I'm making Denver omelettes."

"That sounds wonderful. I'll have one."

"You will?" Marcie had been expecting a fight, and she cocked her round face to one side in wary disbelief.

"Yes. I'm starved. Who stayed over? It looks like you have a crowd for breakfast."

"The Blanchards, for one. But they just arrived. They jog along the beach every morning and stop off here to eat." Marcie tried to sound annoyed at that, but she was secretly pleased that the neighbors preferred her cooking to that of any other cook on the strand. "And then there's the Montgomerys. They didn't sleep over, either. Just showed up as picture perfect as you please, ready to go sailing. Old man Montgomery looks like a commodore in his navy blues."

"The Montgomerys? Do I know them, Marcie? The name is so . . . Jerald? Is there a Jerald with them?"

"A young man is with them, yes. Looks like a porcelain statue, all primped and spiffed in his sailing outfit."

"Sailing outfit?" Adrianna felt her stomach drop as the memory she hadn't bothered to keep slowly reappeared, a memory of herself last night saying something to someone about sailing. In a flash it all came back. She had been barefooted on the lawn, half listening to Jerald as she eyed her bedroom window as a sanctuary of promised relief. "Oh, no! I think I promised I would go sailing with him today. Oh, Marcie, look at me!"

"Did you or didn't you?" she asked.

"I don't remember."

"Then you have nothing to worry about. Play it by ear. Where are you planning to go? To a rodeo?" She smiled as she eyed Adrianna's outfit, nodding silent approval at how beautiful she looked.

"To the track. I bought a racehorse yesterday."

"Horses! You're just as loony as your uncle. Go sailing and forget about horses. I hear these Montgomerys are as wealthy as they come," Marcie said, turning back to her stove.

"You sound more and more like Uncle every time I see you."

"Oh?" Marcie busied herself cracking eggs into a bowl.

"I'm here just to get a horse. I hope to be on my way home by tonight."

"What's your rush? What's one more day?"

"Marcie, you don't understand," Adrianna said, walking up behind her.

"And I never will. You young people are in such a hurry. A nice-looking young man out there waiting to take you for a ride on his boat and you have to rush off to your farm. I don't understand it, Adrianna. And please don't explain it to me. I don't *want* to understand it."

"He's a nice enough young man, I suppose," Adrianna explained. "I could go sailing with him, and his parents, if that would make you happy."

The woman's eyes lit up, and Adrianna struggled not to break into a smile.

"Adrianna," Marcie said, turning away from her eggs to look her in the eyes. "You're . . . you're . . . hopeless."

"What on earth do you mean?"

"You should be planning a wedding, not buying horses. What are you waiting for?"

"Why is everyone in this house so eager to marry me off?"

"It's none of my business," Marcie said, whipping the eggs with a wooden spoon. "I don't want to talk about it. What business is it of mine if you waste your life hoping for love to come barreling down the pike to knock you off your feet? Being in love is like having a sickness. It's something awful. It knots you up inside. You can't sleep. You can't eat. You can't remember things. It's like having amnesia all over your body. It's just awful."

"Oh? Tell me more," Adrianna said, putting her arm around the woman's shoulder.

"When it happens, you'll know it. There is always something unexpected about it, like being struck by lightning on a sunny day."

"You make it sound so . . . so fatalistic."

"Random is the word. As random as a toss of the dice. Don't bet on it, child. Build a secure life with someone like . . ."

"Like Jerald Montgomery?"

"Like Jerald Montgomery. Who knows, somewhere along the way lightning may strike."

"What if it doesn't?"

"What have you lost finding out? A few days away from the farm?"

"But I don't want to get married, Marcie."

"You don't know what you want, girl. All I say is, stay open. Things change so quickly from one day to the next. One day you're buying a horse, the next day . . . who knows?"

One day I'm buying a horse, and the same night I'm on the rooftop of a Victorian mansion in the arms of a total stranger.

"How big do you want your omelette?"

"What? Oh, no food, Marcie. I . . . I thought I was hungry, but I'm not."

Just thinking of him looming in the shadows of her thoughts—huge, powerful, dangerous as a nightmare, yet so warm—made the emptiness inside her crystallize once again into an ache that threatened to sap her strength.

"What's the matter, dear?"

"Nothing . . . nothing. I really don't want to go sailing."

"Just take life as it comes. If you stay a few more days, I promise I won't badger you with a lot of foolish advice." Marcie dropped the spoon in the eggs and kissed Adrianna on the forehead. "Now scat. I've got work to do."

Uncle Alex stood up to greet her, beaming like a proud parent. He seated her next to Jerald and introduced her to the Montgomerys with more than his usual deference to decorum and etiquette. Marcie was right. Old man Montgomery did look like a commodore in his blue sailing blazer and white ascot. Mrs. Montgomery was warm and friendly, casually attired in white duck slacks that contrasted sharply with the elegance and charm of her demeanor. She was the type of woman who could wear a potato sack and still look chic and well dressed. Jerald wore the short-sleeved striped sailing shirt of the deckhand, which made him look all of nineteen. The Blanchards were in matching jogging suits, and Alex, the prince in his castle, reigned supreme in his beige cashmere bathrobe.

Alex directed the topic of conversation towards her, and as Adrianna fielded the questions one by one she got the distinct impression that she was on trial. Mr. and Mrs. Montgomery did all the drilling, while

the Blanchards hung on the periphery, interjecting
comments and anecdotes into every break in the
conversation.

An omelette was placed in front of Adrianna, but
before she could protest, she saw a small card lying
next to it on the same plate. It read simply, "Eat
It!—Marcie." It was something her mother would
have done. Maybe she should go sailing with the
Montgomerys after all—just to please that endearing
pest out in the kitchen.

If Adrianna was on trial, she passed the examination with flying colors. The Montgomerys had a
wonderful way of making her feel at ease. Jerald, she
discovered, was in his last year at Harvard Business
School and was eagerly awaiting induction into the
family business.

"We're sailing to Bridgeport this afternoon, Adrianna," Mrs. Montgomery said, "and we'd be de-
lighted if you would come along."

"Is that in the Bahamas?"

"No, no, child," Alex laughed, slapping his knee.
"Connecticut. Just across the Sound. That is the
Bridgeport you mean, is it not?" he asked the Mont-
gomerys.

"We go to the Bahamas in the winter, Adrianna,
when all that sun and heat does the most good," Mrs.
Montgomery said. "Though sailing down that far is
more work than it is fun. It's best to fly and have the
boat meet you there. Jerald usually takes it down for
us each year."

"The crew sails it down, Mother," Jerald said. "I
merely go along for the ride."

"Don't be so modest. You're a fine sailor," she
retorted.

"The crew?" Adrianna couldn't help herself.

"The *Midnight Sun,* that's the name of the boat, is a little more than a boat, actually," Jerald said. "It's closer to a ship. A hundred and thirty feet long, with a permanent crew of five to maintain and run it."

Her astonishment must have shown on her face, as Mrs. Montgomery leaned over and whispered for everyone to hear, "I call it an aircraft carrier, my dear, but Carlton here"—indicating her husband— "thinks it isn't large enough. If he gets anything bigger, we're going into the oil-tanker business."

Mr. Montgomery quipped back, and in a moment he had the table enthralled, listening to him retell an adventure he had when he first purchased the yacht in Europe and sailed it across the Atlantic ten years ago.

Adrianna picked at her omelette. While her thoughts were distracted by the conversation, she had eaten most of it before she even realized it. *It is better to have something in your stomach before going sailing,* she told herself, even though she hadn't yet made up her mind to accept their invitation.

While one servant was clearing the dishes, another one entered the veranda with a box and placed it in front of Adrianna.

"This just arrived for you, miss," he said.

"For me?" She looked at the Montgomerys and thought how nice it was of them to bring a gift, but they were as perplexed as everyone else. "Was there a note?"

"No, miss," the servant said and left.

It was a plain department-store gift box, un-wrapped, with her name written across the lid.

"I don't understand. Who would send me a gift? Uncle Alex? Are you in one of your gift-giving moods again?"

"That's not from me. I'd have it wrapped, at least."

She placed the lid on the table. The tissue paper inside was neatly folded and held closed by a small gold sticker. She broke the seal and lifted the paper off a pair of shoes. Her shoes! She held them up for everyone to see and then looked into the living room. She could feel Garret's presence as if he were there watching her.

"How lovely," Mrs. Montgomery said. "Look, there's a note in the toe."

"Shoes? Now who would send you a pair of shoes?" Mr. Montgomery said and added, "Especially a pair that has been worn. Look at the bottom. They're scuffed."

"They're mine," Adrianna said. "I . . . I . . . lost them last night."

"Read the note, Adrianna," Mrs. Montgomery babbled excitedly.

"Lost them?" Mrs. Blanchard wondered out loud. She would have asked how someone loses a pair of shoes if Alex hadn't touched her hand to stop her.

The note simply said, "See you soon." It was written on the back of a one-day pass to the stable area of the track. So he wanted her to go to the track. What better reason was there to go sailing now? But that would mean staying over another night.

"What does it say?" Mrs. Montgomery asked.

What could she say? How was it possible to explain to them the circumstances of her losing her shoes? It was none of their business, but it had gone this far and some explanation was necessary.

Alex gave her a knowing look and waited to see how she was going to handle this situation.

"Perhaps it's private and we should all contain our curiosity," Jerald said.

His remark provided an avenue of escape, and Adrianna took it, tucking the shoes back into the box.

"It's all so silly, really. A friend returning a pair of shoes."

That explanation satisfied no one, she knew. But she replaced the lid as if it were all the explanation she was going to give. Feeling awkward and not knowing what else to do, she excused herself and hurried into the house.

"Adrianna!" Jerald called after her, catching up with her on the stairs. "I want to apologize if anything I or my family said . . ."

"Your parents are a dream, and thank you for what you said out there. I'm the one that should apologize. I had completely forgotten our date to go sailing. You probably guessed that by the way I'm dressed. There's just so much that I have to do, Jerald, that—"

"Hey, it's okay. Some other time, then?"

"I'll be leaving tonight to go back home. It's been really nice meeting you." She held out her hand to shake his. "Please make up some excuse to your parents for me. I really like them. I feel so terrible, having put them to all this trouble."

"No trouble at all. I can tell that they enjoyed meeting you."

"You're sweet. See ya," she said, smiling, and then ran up the stairs.

"It's that reporter, isn't it?" he called up to her.

She turned at the head of the stairs and smiled. She didn't answer him. She couldn't. She couldn't admit that to herself, much less to anyone else.

Adrianna drove the sports car her uncle had given her two years ago as a graduation gift. She had refused it when he'd first presented it to her, saying it was too expensive and totally inappropriate for the farm. A pickup truck would have been the better choice, something more useful. But Alex was adamant. He wasn't going to have any niece of his driving around in a farm implement. What would his neighbors think?

"And what would my neighbors think, Uncle, if I come tooling down the country road in this snappy foreign job?" she had retorted.

"You don't give a hoot what your neighbors think. It's your father you're worried about. Afraid to embarrass him because he couldn't afford to buy it for you. Right?"

"Right! And now I can only wonder why you bought it for me."

"Keep the car here and don't tell him a thing. I'll have the thrill of having given you something nice, he'll be spared the embarrassment because he'll never know, and you'll have the pleasure of driving something almost as beautiful as you. Agreed?"

"Your logic is impossible."

"Impeccable is the word, child. Impeccable."

And so was the car. A red Italian convertible surging with power and prestige. The resonance of its engine idling at the stable entrance-gate turned more than a few heads. The guard tipped his hat and let her drive through without asking to see her pass.

She parked under a shady tree alongside a horse trailer and asked the first person she saw where the Worthington stables were. Her uncle's stables were in the opposite direction, and she entertained the thought of visiting them. It had been years since she was there, and although she had a strong recollection of who the trainers and handlers were, she couldn't remember their names. Some other time.

Being in the stable area on a race day was like being backstage during a Broadway production. The air trembled with excitement. Horses readied to go on snorted out the tension building up in their lungs and stomped their forelegs impatiently into the dust. It was the nervous restlessness that Adrianna felt keenly and always responded to. Like actors, these horses, surrounded by a pampering entourage, listened to instructions that they could never understand over the thundering of their own hearts.

She was in no hurry. She strolled slowly through the maze of stables, stopping often to stroke a horse's forehead and coo something soothing and complimentary into its ear. The stable boys milling about never questioned her presence, just smiled their appreciation for the moment's break they took as they stopped to watch her.

She couldn't wait to see Sarazen, but today something else was stirring her appreciation. She watched the occasional cars drive slowly by as the well-dressed strangers got out to inspect some horse or another. Owners. She couldn't imagine Garret as an owner. He didn't fit the type, she thought, knowing full well how illogical that was as she thought about it. Yet, how would he get a pass to the stables? Maybe he was a gambler? Or worse. Some irresponsible playboy. But that didn't jell either. He seemed too smart to be a gambler and too serious to be a playboy. Anyway, she wasn't here to see him. With any luck, she wouldn't see him at all.

She turned a corner and saw a small office bungalow with a sign above its door: Worthington. Behind it were the stables, and in the fourth stall down, she spotted her horse. Sarazen. The white diamond on his forehead, against the ebony black silk of his face, was like a jewel on velvet. She approached him cautiously, sensing the awesome power in the stallion's alert eyes and muscled jowls. He flared his nostrils at her and raised his head in warning. He was studying her every move. She stopped a few feet away to allow him a good whiff of her scent.

"Oh, my, but you are a handsome devil," she whispered. "Oh, Sarazen!"

Was there anything on earth more beautiful? She wondered, struck by the sheer beauty of the animal.

"Are you going to allow me to come closer, or are you going to play hard to get?" she said softly.

He lowered his head in response and stomped a hoof against the wooden planks of his stall.

"I'll assume that's an invitation," she said, trying desperately not to alarm the animal with her trepidation. He whinnied softly and shook his forelock off to the side of his head. "Better to see me with?" she said, stepping slowly up to the stall and beneath the animal's head. He dropped his muzzle into her hair and nudged her away. Again he whinnied, but softer. "Are you calming down? In a while I'm going to reach up and stroke your face. No rush. Just telling you beforehand so there's no misunderstanding."

Whatever doubts she'd had about buying this horse had now vanished. She knew in her heart that she had done the right thing.

"Hey you, lady, get away from that horse!"

A man in work clothes and a hat was walking briskly towards her. His yelling startled her and, in turn, Sarazen, who grunted loudly and began tossing his head in violent disapproval. Adrianna had to step back to avoid being hit by his powerful head.

"What do you think you're doing? Get away from that horse! He'll take a bite out of you!"

"How dare you scare me like that!" Adrianna said, exasperated that she was interrupted at such a critical moment. "We were getting along just fine until you— you frightened us!"

"Don't tell me my business, miss. That horse is one mean hombre, and you have no business being here. So, vamoose!"

He was a smallish man with a grizzled beard and a cigar stub stuck in the corner of his mouth. His wide-brimmed hat was cocked to the back of his head, revealing his sparse gray hair. He looked as if he had worked the stables his entire life. *He should know better than to yell like that around horses,* she thought.

"I have all the right in the world to be here. For your information, I claimed this horse yesterday. Do you work here?"

"Claimed him? You claimed Sarazen? I don't know anything about that. You'll have to talk to the boss."

"Indeed. And where is the boss?"

"Right that way," he said, pointing towards the office. "Sorry I scared you. Just doing my job."

"No harm done, I hope. It'll take me a little longer now to win back Sarazen's confidence."

"He needs a good clout, is all. Works every time."

"A good clout?" Adrianna couldn't believe her ears. She had to bite her lip to keep from yelling. She took a breath to keep her composure and stared daggers into his eyes. "That horse is mine now, and don't you forget it. If I see you as much as frown at him, I'll . . . I'll . . ." There was a riding crop hanging from a nail on a post nearby. She grabbed it and held it up to his face. ". . . I'll skin you alive!"

He took a step back, spit the cigar stub out at his feet, turned and walked away.

What a despicable little creature, Adrianna thought. She slapped her boots with the crop to punctuate her anger and stormed off towards the office. She would have Sarazen moved to her uncle's stalls immediately, and she'd give the boss an earful about his hired help. Armed with the crop and fueled by the anger still pumping adrenaline through her veins, she opened the office door, stood with her hands on her hips and targeted the man sitting behind the desk. His back was turned. He was on the phone, leaning back in his chair with his feet propped up against the wall.

The office was one large room lined on all four sides with photographs, old hitches, stirrups, horseshoes— paraphernalia packed tightly together like a collage built up randomly over many years. The planked flooring was bare except for the layer of grist, ground into a fine powdery salt that seemed to bleach the wood almost white. A large leather-bound sofa against a wall had a horse blanket crumpled on it as if someone had spent the night there. The massive antique desk in the center dominated the room. It bore its scratches and scars proudly, like awards won for having survived years of hard work.

The rangy black hair of the man sitting behind it should have clued her, but Adrianna was too preoccupied by her impatient anger. When he turned to hang up the phone, she slapped her boots again with the crop and almost began by introducing herself.

"Close the door," he said, standing up. His presence took command of the room and everything in it. His leather vest and rolled-up sleeves attested somehow to his right of ownership; his broad smile and sparkling eyes dispelled her anger and, along with it, every notion she had of telling him off.

"Garret!"

Chapter Five

"Close the door," he said again. It was more of an invitation than a command. She hesitated as she felt the trepidation his presence evoked from her. Fighting to regain her poise, she pushed the door shut.

"Coffee?" On a table to his right was an electric coffeepot and an odd collection of mugs. As she watched him pour, she noted to herself that this was the third time they had met and each time he was dressed in a totally different style. She couldn't imagine that he ever looked better. The muscles of his forearms were rigidly packed, not thick from artificial exercise, but tempered tight and hard from constant use. His hands looked rougher than she remembered them, but she had never studied them before, just felt them as they closed around her waist or when his fingers touched her cheeks. His faded blue denim shirt hugged his chest and tapered in to his waist, which was cinched by a thick belt. The leather vest, thin and softened by age, followed the contours of his shoulders and upper back. His slacks were work pants, but like everything else he wore, they too stressed a power and potency as they hugged his lean thighs.

"What are you doing here?" she finally said, knowing at once how outrageous that must sound to him. He looked completely at home, as if he belonged there.

"I'd guess you take your coffee with a dash of cream and no sugar," he said, filling the two cups and waiting with a small carton of cream in his hand.

Why hadn't he said he was connected to Worthington Stables? *Why the charade,* she thought as she studied his face for a clue, a sign that he knew he had made a fool of her. But his smile wasn't a triumphant one, or it didn't seem so to Adrianna. Somehow she must have answered him, because he poured some cream into her cup, walked out from behind the desk and handed her the mug.

"Have a seat." He indicated the couch for her and sat himself on the edge of the desk. "I like the crop. Nice touch. Makes you look more indignant."

"Why didn't you tell me that you were . . . connected with Worthington Stables?" she asked.

"Connected? I'm the head trainer. Have been for the past three years." He took a sip of his coffee. "Taste it. It's good."

"Head trainer?"

"Don't sound so shocked." He smiled. "I'm damn good at it, too."

"Then you know all there is to know about Sarazen?"

"Raised him from a colt."

Much as she hated to admit it, Adrianna was impressed. She realized that trainers were the heart and soul of thoroughbred racing, and a good one was worth his weight in gold.

"Why didn't you tell me?" She sat up on the edge of the couch, not knowing which emotion, anger or frustration, she should vent on him first.

"Did you get your shoes back? I went back up to the lookout to get them and ended up staying there for a while. I watched you talking with Jerald on the lawn."

Yes, she remembered the sensation of being watched, but she hadn't seen him. Strange that she would feel his presence without seeing him. But perhaps it wasn't so strange, she thought as she eyed his long legs and the coarse-grained ruggedness of his clothes that matched his overpowering virility.

"Yes, I got them back at breakfast, with a table full of people. It was embarrassing, to say the least. Jerald and his parents were there."

"He doesn't waste time, does he?"

"What do you mean?"

"Having you meet his parents. He must have been taken with you. Can't say that I blame him. Have you decided what you'd like to have for dinner tonight?" He folded his arms across his chest, and it seemed to her that for one vainglorious moment he relished his self-satisfaction. She wasn't going to let him dwell on it.

"You're the one who doesn't waste much time. Dinner is out of the question. I told you last night that I would be on my way home by tonight."

"So you did. Well," he said, standing up and taking her coffee cup out of her hand, "that doesn't give me much time to change your mind." He put her cup on the desk, grabbed her by the shoulders and pulled her up.

"What do you think you're doing?"

"Changing your mind."

"Don't try it," she said as his powerful hands moved down her arms, pinning her elbows to her side. A subtle scent of cologne churned up the memories of last night, and the sensation of his hands touching her initiated a trembling in her legs. He had to stiffen his hold to steady her.

He looked at her as if to ask if she was okay. No, she wasn't okay. His arms were a vise, a trap that would ignite those feelings she was trying desperately to contain. The best defense was no defense. As she watched him in that moment, she could only pray he didn't sense how vulnerable she really was. His eyes traced her neck and then the swell of her breasts as if he, too, had to make a decision, one he didn't like to make. The intensity slowly went out of his eyes. He let her go and sat back on the edge of the desk.

"You can't just run away like this. Not now."

"I'm not running away," she said. She felt light-headed and had an urge to run now that he had freed her from his grasp. "I'm just getting my horse and going back home."

"You're not doing anything of the kind," he said. "Sarazen . . ." He stood up, took a deep breath and walked across the room. "Sarazen isn't ready to travel yet. You'll have to allow him to recuperate from his race yesterday."

"I was just outside looking at him. He seems fine to me."

"He's too spirited a horse to be locked up inside a trailer for any length of time. He'd have to be tranquilized. I don't want to drug him just yet."

"I'll be the judge of that," Adrianna said, feeling bolder now that there was some distance between them.

"You'll judge nothing, young lady," he snapped.

The sudden violence in his voice caused her to take a step backwards. "No one knows more about that horse than I do. He travels when I say he's ready to travel, and not before." He took a few steps towards her but stopped when she backed away and stumbled against the desk. "Look," he said, his voice soft and almost pleading, "I'm not lying to you."

"Is this just a ploy to keep me here? I seem to remember you promising to do something drastic if I wouldn't have dinner with you."

He thought a moment and then almost laughed when he remembered the scene. "No. Drastic is storming into the house, throwing a blanket over you and hauling you off."

"You wouldn't dare!" He was joking, she thought, but he said nothing, allowing her to make of it whatever she wished. No doubt he was capable of doing it. He was the type of man who could do anything he put his mind to. It was this realization that triggered the memory she had tried to suppress. She remembered how determined he looked last night when he said that he got what he wanted, and that he wanted . . . her.

"Sarazen is not ready to travel. That's simple enough to understand."

"Maybe. But certainly he's capable of being walked over to the Trent stables."

He hadn't expected that. She congratulated herself as she watched him take in the information. He raised his eyebrows, acknowledging that she had a point, but he wasn't going to give in that easily. "Sure, he could be moved to Trent's stalls, but unless the ownership is properly transferred, his insurance would be ineffective. If something should happen to him over there, our insurance company wouldn't pay and neither would your uncle's."

Adrianna had no idea if he was telling her the truth or not. It sounded reasonable enough, even though she could sense he was stretching to make a point.

"Well then, let's transfer the papers. I've got the money to pay for him right here," she said, slapping the pocket of her jeans. But suddenly she remembered that she didn't have the money. She had left it at the house. She was going to give it to Alex in exchange for his personal check. She had forgotten to do that, what with the Montgomerys showing up for breakfast and then her haste to get out of the house.

"Sarazen was claimed by Alex Trent. You sure don't look like Alex Trent to me."

"A formality. I'm his niece."

"Some formality," he said, eyeing her entire body from head to toe. "I think it's impossible you could convince anyone you're not a young . . . attractive . . . totally captivating female gold digger, probably taking the old boy for every dime he's got."

"I've convinced you."

"Have you? That woman I was with last night was more exciting than any ten women I've ever known."

"Really?" Coming from him, that was a compliment, even though it wasn't meant to be. Or was it? He was smiling, and she sensed that he might be pulling her leg. "Cut the bull, Garret. You're stalling."

"Maybe. But you're being unreasonable. I'm trying to do what's best for my . . . for the horse. Let him stay in familiar surroundings, and let me see to his health. You would want him certified in perfect health, wouldn't you, before you take legal possession of him?"

"Of course. But . . ."

"But nothing. What's another day? Use your head. If Trent has a mare in heat over there, Sarazen will kick down his stall. He'd have to be restrained. I don't like my horses chained up."

The concern was evident in his eyes. He thought of Sarazen as his horse, a sign that he put more of himself into his job than was necessary. She liked that possessive nature of his. It inspired trust and honesty. Sarazen would indeed be better off under his control.

"He's a real dynamo?"

"A powerhouse of a stallion," he said, shaking his head at the thoughts crowding in behind his eyes. "Too much horse for one little filly like you to get hold of."

"Don't let the size fool you. I've been around horses all my life."

"You've never been around anything like him." He wasn't trying to scare her. His words were spoken with such emotion she could sense he was upset about losing the horse. "Let's go have a look." He took a bridle off the wall and held the door open for her.

If he was so attached to Sarazen, then why had he entered him in that claiming race? She made a mental note to ask him about it at the most opportune moment.

When they stepped out onto the porch, she spotted the sinister-looking man who had startled her and Sarazen. He was now leaning into the window of a limousine, talking to someone in the backseat.

"Who is that?" Adrianna asked.

"Worthington. The owner, dear lady, the owner," he said with more than a trace of sarcasm.

"That scruffy little man is Worthington?"

"No, no. Worthington is in the car. That's Floyd Hess. My assistant."

"He yelled at me to get away from Sarazen before. He said Sarazen needed a good clout."

"Oh? He did, did he? Those two never got along.

Sarazen bit him the very first time he laid eyes on him."

"And no wonder. I don't like him, either. I told him if he even looks at Sarazen, I'm going to skin him alive."

"Ha! That's the spirit. But believe me, Sarazen doesn't need your protection. The person who hits him wouldn't live long enough to tell about it."

As she followed Garret to the stalls, she noticed Floyd Hess watching them. She couldn't see Worthington in the backseat; the car's interior was too dark. Just as Floyd seemed to be about to call out to them, a hand from within the car rested on his arm to restrain him. A woman's hand. Garret had noticed it also, but he kept on walking. It was no business of hers what the relationship was between Floyd Hess and Worthington, or between them and Garret for that matter. She could only wonder at Garret's determination not to acknowledge them.

"How close did Sarazen let you get to him?" Garret said, grabbing her elbow and steering her towards the stalls.

"I was right up to the gate. We were getting along just fine."

"He must like you. He's usually very wary of strangers."

"I have a way with animals," she said, looking up into his face.

"I bet you do. You have a nice disposition," he explained, "that animals would pick up on. Let's just see how well Sarazen takes to you."

As they neared the stalls, he handed her the bridle and asked her to wait by the hitching post. He then approached the stall and whistled softly. Sarazen tossed his head in recognition. Garret drew back the bolt on the gate, turned his back to the horse and walked out into the middle of the road.

"No sharp movements, now," he called to Adrianna. "I'm going to signal him to come out."

"You don't have the bridle on him," she said. "How will you restrain him if he . . . ?"

"I won't have to if you don't panic him." Garret looked up and down the road. The limo and Floyd Hess were gone. They were alone.

Garret whistled sharply between his teeth, and Sarazen tossed his head.

"Come on, big feller," he called and then whistled a soft, melodic birdcall. The horses in the other stalls also responded, watching Garret attentively as if he were calling them. Sarazen lifted his large head into the air and whinnied loudly. Adrianna leaned into the post and thought the horse was going to rear up on his hind legs. "Easy, Adrianna," Garret said, "nothing to worry about. Come on, big guy, push the gate open."

Sarazen kicked the gate open, and Adrianna stepped behind the post in case he decided to charge. But he just stepped out of his stall and shook his head. His nostrils flared, drawing in the air around him like a furnace sucking in oxygen, stoking up the internal fire that powered his muscular machine.

The horse was larger than Adrianna had imagined. Sunlight glistened off the rich ebony hide in waves of blue and purple sheen. He stopped alongside Adrianna, quietly turned and bowed his head towards her.

"Well now, isn't that something?" Garret said. "Beauty and the Beast. Don't move yet. He's trying to win you over with those big sad eyes of his. Don't fall for it. He'll break your heart."

Oh, but he did win her over. It was all she could do not to reach out and touch him. His eyes were bottomless black pools too gentle and soft to belong to such a powerful animal. She held her breath, and in a moment of wordless communication she was totally mesmerized by him.

"That's enough, big guy. She's impressed. Come on over here."

And like a tame pet, the black Arabian walked slowly over and nudged his forehead into Garret's chest. "Yeah, I know she's pretty," he said to him as he wrapped his arms around the horse's face and hugged him. "But I saw her first. I'm going to introduce you two, but you behave yourself, you hear? Go ahead, get your sugar. I keep a sugar stick inside my vest for him," he called to Adrianna. "You can come over now. But don't walk up behind him. Give him a nice wide arc so he can get a good look at you."

Adrianna walked slowly out into the street, noting the magnificent animal as only a horseman could. Neck and shoulders proportioned to the body, sharply muscled and not bulky; long forearms and short cannons; prominent withers, not thick and rounding; supple pasterns, set at a good angle; back straight; fetlocks cleanly cut; loin firmly muscled and ribs well sprung. She could study that animal for days and not know all there was to know of him. He was dazzling, the most majestic animal she had ever seen.

Sarazen knew just where to look as he worked his muzzle inside Garret's vest and plucked out the brown stick of sugar. What a picture the two of them made, she thought.

"Here she comes, so you be nice, you hear?"

She thought it extraordinary that a man would talk to a horse. She had always felt men and horses were indifferent to each other, like two people doing a job who tolerated each other's presence for the sake of the work that had to be done. Yet she could see in the way Garret looked at that animal that there was more than just the natural pride of being associated with something splendidly beautiful. The way he hugged Sarazen's head and rubbed his cheek against his face was evidence of a special bond between them, one that was built on something more than mutual respect.

"Sarazen, this is Adrianna. Adrianna, this is the best-looking animal you'll ever live to see. And he knows it, too. Go ahead, touch him."

She stroked his nose and the hard muscled bone of his forehead. "I think this is what Nature had in mind when she decided to build a horse," she said.

"Well said. If you treat him right, he'll learn to trust you. Try to put the bridle on him."

"I'll never reach the top of his head," she said.

"Well?" he said, looking Sarazen in the face as if he should understand the problem. Without another word from Garret, Sarazen lowered his head, and Adrianna slipped the bridle over his nose and back behind his ears.

"How did you make him do that?" she asked. "He couldn't understand . . . ?"

"I don't know what he understands," he said. "He never ceases to amaze me. There are days when I think he understands everything I say to him, every word."

"You talk to all your horses?"

"Yeah, I guess I do. Silly, isn't it?"

"I don't think so. It's a good way to soothe them. You have a nice disposition that animals pick up on," she said, repeating what he had said to her earlier.

"Four-legged or two-legged?"

"I'd say from what I can gather that you do pretty well with the four-legged kind."

"What about the two-legged ones?" She couldn't answer him. She felt she was going to blush, and as she looked away, Sarazen jerked his head and snorted.

"Thank you, Sarazen, my sentiments exactly," she said.

"Ganging up on me already?" Garret laughed, tugging the bridle strap along Sarazen's cheek. "He's a sucker for a pretty face. I knew I couldn't trust him."

"Maybe he's just emulating his trainer's behavior?" Adrianna said, patting the horse's nose and feeling Garret's eyes studying her.

"Maybe. I didn't think he'd take to you so readily. He must sense that you really like him. Animals have a way of knowing if they are liked or not."

"You didn't want him to like me, did you?" she said, surprised that the words just leaped out of her mouth before she could think of them.

"I didn't expect you to like him as much as you obviously do. It's stupid, I know, but I . . ."

"But you're attached to him, and you don't want to see him go?"

He looked at her and didn't answer. His eyes betrayed his feelings, and he turned back to the horse.

"Yes," he said, studying the horse's forehead, his rough hands gently rubbing the soft skin under its eyes. "Yes, I don't want to see him go. Here," he said, taking her hand and placing the palm under Sarazen's eye, "he loves it when you rub him softly right there. Remember that," he said, and took her hand away. "I'd better put him back before some car comes along and spooks him."

He slipped the bridle off the horse and put it over his shoulder. He gently cupped the horse's mouth with both hands and looked him straight in the eyes. "Now, do this right, you hear? You made a big hit so far, so don't blow it. I'm going to let you go back all by yourself. I know you can do it."

As Garret spoke, Sarazen lowered his head and pressed his forehead into Garret's chest. When he was given the command to go, he swung his nose over to Adrianna and brushed it against her shoulder. He backed up and swung his head high into the air, lifting his front legs a foot or two off the ground.

"Garret?" Adrianna said, alarmed, grabbing onto his arm.

"It's okay. He's just showing off. Go on! Get back to your stall!"

Sarazen beat the road with his forelegs and pranced into a full circle, the muscles in his shoulders quivering, threatening to propel him into a gallop.

"That's very nice," Garret said, standing in a scolding position with his hands on his hips. "We can see how beautiful you are. Now go back home."

With that, Sarazen turned, and with all the exuberance and joy of life, he high-stepped back into his stall.

"Bravo! I thought you trained horses to race?" Adrianna said, surprised at how responsive Sarazen was to verbal commands. "Have you ever thought about the circus?" she joked.

"You put that horse in a circus, lady, and I'll shoot him," he said calmly, as if he were relating a simple fact, something he had determined a long time ago.

"I wouldn't think of it," she said, jarred by the tension that suddenly crystallized the air between them.

He locked the stall, patted the horse one more time and took Adrianna by the arm. "Where's your car?"

"Oh? Am I leaving?"

"Yes. I've got work to do. Two horses running today. One in the eighth and one in the ninth."

"I won't get in your way."

"Some of the men around here are superstitious about having a female around before a race. They think it's bad luck."

She stopped and pulled her arm away. "And what do you think?"

"I think I have enough to do without worrying about the morale of my men. I'll walk you to your car. Where are you parked?"

She knew she wasn't going to change his mind. There was nothing she could do anyway, now that Sarazen was going to stay put for at least another day. "I'm near the gate, under the trees. Don't bother. I can manage."

"No bother. We haven't decided where we're going to have dinner tonight. I thought we could discuss it on the way."

"Discuss it? That's a new one. Since when do you discuss anything? I thought for sure you'd have the reservations made by now at your favorite spot."

"Without asking you?" He smiled.

"Why ask? The word no doesn't mean anything to you. You'd just come to the house, throw a blanket over me and trundle me off—right?"

He laughed heartily, and she was relieved to see the merriment back in his eyes.

"That was merely a threat, not a promise. But whatever turns you on."

"You're outrageous, Garret. Your only saving grace is your kindness toward Sarazen."

"Okay, we'll try it your way one more time," he said, stopping and grabbing her by the shoulders. "Since you won't be leaving to go back home tonight, and since you are going to eat dinner anyway, why don't we have dinner together?" *So far, so good.* "And if you tell me no one more time, I will wrap you in a blanket and hang you on my office wall. Dare me!" he said, and he grabbed her around the waist as if to carry her off.

"Stop! Okay!"

"I knew eventually I'd get through to you," he teased. "Eight o'clock okay?"

"You tell me!" she said sarcastically.

"Okay. Eight o'clock. I'll be by at seven-thirty. I want to talk with Alex Trent about last night. I owe him an apology."

"No need. I apologized for you already."

"No one can apologize for someone else, little lady."

"Too bad, I already did. And I don't want you to pick me up. Tell me where the place is and I'll meet you there."

"You've got a lot of spunk, you know that?"

"You bring out the best in me," she said.

"And you bring out the worst in me. I can't remember ever feeling so compelled to always play it rough with someone. What is it with you? I've never had so much trouble with anyone in all my life." The exasperation in his voice didn't match the admiration for her that sparkled in his eyes. He stepped out quickly, and she almost had to jog to keep up. "Which one's yours?" he said, eyeing the cars under the trees. "Don't tell me. Let me guess. Not the coupe. Not the sedan. Of course. The perfect car to match your fiery temper." He opened the door of the red sports car for her and smiled. "If this isn't your car, it should be."

"It is," she said, getting in behind the wheel.

He took a business card from his wallet, wrote the directions on it, and handed it to her.

"Eight o'clock. And don't be late," he warned, leaning on the door.

"What if I stand you up?" She waited for his reaction to register in his eyes. He leaned closer, and for a moment she thought he was going to kiss her.

"I'll come after you."

Although there was a smile on his lips, the steel blue eyes carried another message that convinced her he would do just that. She hoped he didn't realize how much it affected her to confront him head-on like this.

"Bring the papers for Sarazen and I'll bring the money," she demanded. "We'll close the deal. Once and for all." She started the engine and turned to look over her shoulder. She didn't want to see how he was going to receive that bit of information. It surprised her that she was able to say it with any degree of authority. All she could think of now was making a clean getaway.

As she drove off towards the gate, she saw him in the rearview mirror, watching her. With his hands on his hips and his head held back, he appeared totally in control of this temporary petulance of hers, as if he had handled situations like this a thousand times before, as if he held the power to control her.

Chapter Six

"Marcie, is Uncle Alex around?"

"Oh, there you are. Yes, dear, he's in the den. I had your bags packed. If you tell me when you'll be leaving, I'll make your dinner. Or would you rather have some sandwiches to take along?"

For a moment Adrianna just watched the elderly woman move about the kitchen, the world she had claimed for herself so many years ago, and wondered why she was finding it so difficult to tell her that she had changed her mind. Or had her mind been changed for her? Marcie would see that. She was as aggravatingly perceptive as Alex. It was sheer folly to hide anything from those knowing eyes of hers. But Adrianna was in no mood to explain. She couldn't. All she knew was that her plans to get Sarazen were now complicated by the one man who, more than anyone she had ever met, had so . . . so . . . unnerved her.

"I'll be staying another day. Some unforeseen technicalities about the horse."

"Nothing serious, I hope?" Marcie said, wiping her hands on her apron and eyeing Adrianna as if setting up the invisible antennae of her intuition.

"No, nothing like that. A formality. Red tape."

"Well, good. I hope those formalities keep you here for a week. Anything I can do?"

"No. Not unless you know anything about insurance and drugging horses for travel."

"You'll have to see your uncle about that." Marcie knew there was something more serious troubling Adrianna, but she didn't probe.

Adrianna could have kissed her for that silent reassurance, and before she knew it, she had her arms around the woman. There was nothing she had to say. Marcie understood when the most profound advice anyone could give was a hug and a kiss.

"Supper's at six. Your favorite. Chicken Kiev."

"I have a dinner date."

"Anyone I know?"

"You know any horse trainers?"

Marcie took a deep breath and sighed. But the scolding look Adrianna expected to find in her eyes never appeared.

"Horses! I don't understand," she said, shaking her head as if she had given up trying.

Neither do I, dear Marcie. Neither do I.

Alex was at his desk behind a pile of papers. He wore a pair of glasses, half-lenses which, perched on the tip of his nose, gave him the unmistakable look of a professor grading tests. Looking over the lenses and out from under those bushy gray eyebrows, he seemed more studious than she had ever remembered him.

"Aha!" he said, placing the paper he was scanning into a manila envelope, "the prodigal niece returns."

"Are you in one of your moods, Uncle? Because if you are, I can come back later." Adrianna wanted to circumvent his anger at her for missing the golden opportunity she had that morning with the Montgomerys.

"Best defense is a good offense, eh? Very good. I wonder where you get that from? Probably me. Sit down," he said, indicating a green leather armchair. He leaned back in his chair and propped his feet up on the desk. "Well? Go on."

She tried to read his expression, but coupled with his gray hair and stout cheeks, his glasses transformed him into a caricature of Saint Nick.

"I'd love to," she said, accepting the invitation to speak her mind. If there was anyone who needed to apologize about breakfast with the Montgomerys, it was him, and she was determined not to allow him to blame her for any embarrassment she might have caused by running off. But his smile drained her of her anger.

"The look on Mrs. Montgomery's face was priceless," he said before she could say another word. "You must have noticed. And old Carlton, miffed and warily perplexed by those shoes—what intrigue must have raced through those pampered blue-blooded minds of theirs. I tell you, I never enjoyed a moment like that in my entire life. Where on earth did you run off to? Young Jerald was almost in convulsions, trying to fumble some excuse to appease the royal lord and lady."

"I thought you'd be upset!"

"Upset? Ha! It serves them right. The nerve of them, barging in here uninvited to impress everyone with their presence."

"I . . . I thought you invited them."

"Invited them? I gave up inviting them to this house years ago. They would never come to one of my parties because, believe it or not, Alex Trent is not listed in the blue book. Jerald invited them."

"I thought they were quite nice, really. I hope I didn't embarrass you."

"You think everybody's nice. Just like your Aunt Frances, God rest her soul. I don't know what got into me, introducing you to Jerald. Good Lord, if you ever married into that family, I'd never see you again. With those impossible in-laws, I'd have to disown you."

"Uncle, you amaze me. Just when I was getting a good fix on you, you change in midstream and go sailing off in a totally different direction."

"Oh? And I'm not allowed the privilege of changing my mind?"

"No, you're not." She laughed, amazed that she'd just blurted that out. "Of course you are. What I mean is, I thought I knew you, and now . . ."

"There's more to this old coot than you imagined?" he teased.

"Something like that."

"Good. I'd hate to be fixed and predictable in anyone's eyes."

"It's the horseman in you. I'm feeling that old familiar tug on the leg. You've got something cooking in that obstinate head of yours. Am I right?"

He took off the glasses, put his hands behind his head and, facing the ceiling, looked back into his thoughts and memories. "No, it's nothing like that. It's just that when I saw you open that box this morning, the look on your face reminded me of your Aunt Frances. There was one moment I could never forget . . . It was her birthday. I had come late, and she was sitting in a gazebo out on the lawn, opening her presents and surrounded by a dozen boyfriends. 'Beaus' was the term we used then. She was so beautiful, she took my breath away. I just stood back and watched her for the longest time. I had nothing to give her. I had rented the suit I wore that day—and I couldn't even pay for that. So, on a whim—I don't know if it was a whim or not—I cornered this little kid, gave him a quarter, and told him to give Miss Frances this ring." He held up his left hand and showed her the small silver ring he wore on his pinky finger.

"My fraternity ring. She must have had a dozen of them already. I expected she would question all those beaus about whose it was and have a good laugh doing so. I'll never forget when that little boy handed it to her. She knew immediately it was from me. She stood up and looked at the people gathered around her. She was looking for me, as if she could sense my presence and she had to find me or lose me forever. I'll never forget it. I saw that look again this morning, when you opened that box."

His eyes were filled with tears. He slowly sat upright in his chair, put his glasses back on the tip of his nose and fussed with some papers on the desk.

"Well? What is it? The way you came barging in here, it could only be about that horse."

She was too moved to talk. That she could elicit such a touching memory from him brought tears to her eyes. Yes, she'd felt his presence this morning, and yes, she'd even looked about her expecting to see him. But it was the implications of that she was now examining. She didn't want to think about it. It was too dangerous. Too much of what she had planned for herself was now too suddenly at risk.

"Uncle, I have the money for the horse, which I'll

give you for a personal check. I don't want anything to go wrong with the transfer."

"Good idea." He found his check ledger under some papers and began to write it out. She wanted to ask him about what Garret had told her—the insurance and the procedure to drug horses for shipment. But she reminded herself that this was her deal and that she was old enough to see it through herself.

"I have the money upstairs," she said, standing up.

"Don't bother with it now," he said. "I wouldn't know where to put it. I won't be going to the bank for another three or four days. Are you leaving tonight?"

"No. Maybe tomorrow. I haven't tied up all the loose ends yet."

He looked at her over his glasses but didn't ask for any further explanations.

"Marcie's making Chicken Kiev."

"I know. I have a date."

His eyebrows lifted in a questioning gesture, but he looked back at his desk and finished filling out the check.

"If you have any problems, if anything comes up about the deal that you don't understand, let me know. I've claimed more horses than I care to think about. Only one in a hundred is any good." He paused to look at her very closely. "You have that one in a hundred?"

Her intuition told her he was referring to something more than just a racehorse.

Three times she changed her clothes, and each time that she examined herself in her floor-length mirror, she found a hundred things wrong with her outfit. She had to remind herself consciously that this date was, after all, a business meeting, and anything distracting would be sabotaging her own interests. *Stay simple and plain, keep to the subject.*

She rethought the possibilities of her simple white sundress and quickly slipped into it again for another look. The neckline was high and the front was ruffled enough to soften the curvature of her breasts. It was the most comfortable, she decided, even though it did accent her tan and impose a breezy island-girl look. The dress extended well below her calves. She wore strapped sandals to match, the heels of which were just high enough to make the outfit appropriate for dining out.

Even if she was dressing to cover as much of herself as she could, she thought, the dress did flatter her small frame and bestow upon her a fresh innocence that she knew some men would find attractive. But not Garret. His was the slinky, black velvet type, and that sudden realization confirmed that she had finally made the right choice about what to wear.

The restaurant, Arpeggio's, was somewhere on the bluffs overlooking Oyster Bay, just past the quaint and idyllic town of Cold Spring Harbor. It wasn't a long drive by any means, but the winding road and the scenic glimpses now and then of the water through the pine and oak trees made Adrianna slow the sports car to a leisurely pace. It was heavenly to emerge from the shadows of trees into the light of a cloudless sunset high up on the ridge and then dip back into the woods as the road wound its way along the coast.

Arpeggio's was a converted New England cottage situated out on an isolated bluff. The setting sun baked the windows facing the water a bright orange, placing the entrance and the decorative brick framed sign in a deep contrasting shadow. The canopy along the walk was lighted well in advance of the approaching night, giving the place a look of welcoming warmth.

Armed with her purse and her uncle's check, Adrianna waited nervously for the valet to park her car before asking him the time. Eight-thirty. A fashionable thirty minutes late. She took off her knitted scarf, puffed her hair in the reflection of the door, and took a deep breath before stepping inside.

The maître d' behind the small reception desk smiled at her. He wore a continental tuxedo which in the confines of the foyer of a New England cottage seemed ostentatious.

"Miss Adams?"

"Yes."

"This way, please."

As she followed him into the main dining room, the simple elegance of the furnishings and table settings upstaged his formal attire. The place had looked deceptively small from the outside. The room was large enough to seat at least a hundred people. The windows overlooking the water were leaded glass set in a pattern of small diamond-shaped crystals, beveled and faintly stained to filter the light. Each window was framed in a tieback curtain that matched the light lavender of the lace tablecloths. The napkins, a dark burgundy, were folded into peaks and stood waiting at attention over each setting of bone china and sculptured silver flatware.

The room was virtually empty. The few diners scattered about were under the spell of softness, the hush of the iridescence from the simple porcelain-and-gold candelabras illuminating each table in its own special alcove of light.

He led her through the room and down the steps into the bar, an English pub of oak and pewter, long wooden tap handles and brass fixtures. One side opened out onto a flower garden and a small, intimate patio of cocktail tables and chairs. Each table had a candle burning under an amber glass. The view was breathtaking. The far horizon glowed red and violet as the setting sun battled majestically against the night, which had reached as far as Connecticut, engulfing the small white lights strung like pearls along the shore.

The maître d' pulled out a padded chair for Adrianna and signaled a waiter standing near the door.

"Champagne? Compliments of the house. Mr. Malone called just before you arrived. He extends his apologies. He'll be along shortly. He thought you would appreciate the view and asked if you would be so kind as to wait for him here."

"How nice. The view is wonderful. Champagne would be lovely."

The waiter listened attentively to the instructions of the maître d'. He gave a small nod and disappeared into the bar.

"Do you know Mr. Malone well? Does he come here often?"

"Mr. Malone is a very good customer," he said, smiling.

"How good?"

"Madame?"

"No. Nothing." What she wanted to know, she couldn't ask directly; besides, the man's formal bearing promised he would be professionally discreet. "Did Mr. Malone say what was detaining him?"

"One of his horses took ill. He had to care for it."

"Sarazen?"

"Madame?"

The waiter returned with a silver ice bucket and the bottle of champagne. The maître d' opened and poured it and, with her permission, excused himself. With a stable full of horses, why would it be Sarazen? If Sarazen were sick, she could think of no one else she would rather have care for him than Garret.

The champagne was excellent. When she took another sip, she glimpsed a man standing in the doorway, watching her. She almost turned, but she forced herself to look out over the water and pretend, as she felt him approach, that she was totally alone with her thoughts.

He stood behind her chair, and his presence electrified the air, tickling the skin behind her neck and raising goose bumps along her arms. She was about to turn when he placed his hands on her shoulders and bent down to whisper in her ear.

"Sorry, unfortunate business. I wouldn't have kept you waiting unless it was an extreme emergency." He kissed her softly on the cheek, and the clean masculine aroma of his cologne evaporated her thoughts. All she knew was how wonderful it felt having him so close to her once again.

He sat down opposite her and held her hands. He looked concerned, though the worry lines around his eyes were slowly beginning to disappear. He wore a tweed sports jacket and a white silk shirt open at the collar. White was such a wonderful contrast to his black hair and tanned skin, framing his handsome face in reflected candlelight.

"Is it Sarazen?" she said. A sudden pang deep inside her intruded into her consciousness, but she knew just by looking at him that it wasn't.

"No. My entry in the eighth. Fargo. Came up limping on the last turn into the stretch. I had his forelegs packed in ice. I'm waiting for the X rays to come back."

"Ligaments?"

"I don't know. If it's serious, he'll have to be destroyed. That's a gamble you take every single day in this business." He sat back for a moment, allowing the weight of his thoughts free reign before he forced them from his mind. "Well, enough of that. Tell me, how do you keep looking so beautiful? Every time I see you, it's like for the first time. I never know what to expect, and you never disappoint me." His eyes raked over her, and he seemed more impressed with how she looked now than he did when she wore the black velvet evening dress.

"Bobby!" he called to the waiter standing by the door. "Cut this beautiful young lady a flower. A yellow one."

Bobby plucked a yellow daylily from the flower beds near the table and handed it to Garret, who stripped the long stem and then slid the flower in behind her ear.

"I know it's supposed to mean something which ear it goes behind, but I've forgotten," he said.

"Do you always dress your dates for dinner?" she said. Maybe it was the way he cleaned the stem, as if he had done it many times before. He sat back out of the light, his eyes glinting as he discovered the challenge in her question.

"No. I usually undress them after dinner."

"I'm not surprised. And what comes off first? The flower, I suppose."

"Oh, no. That's last," he said, the sarcasm in his voice overriding the humor suddenly so alive in his eyes. "The flower I gently press into her hands afterwards. As a keepsake. A souvenir of the evening."

"How romantic. Sounds almost foolproof. You must have had a lot of success with it."

"Lots. It's been tested out at . . . oh, ninety percent efficiency. Not bad, considering the hundreds of fair damsels who have been selectively chosen for the experiment."

"Oh, experiment, is it? What an interesting word. And have you chosen me . . . for an experiment?"

"Of course. But deep down, I just knew the flower trick wasn't going to do it." As she gently touched the flower, she wished she had said nothing about it at all.

"Switch to plan B?" she said.

"Yes, plan B." He sat forward and touched her hand. "More champagne?"

"I should refuse. Why make it any easier for you?"

"Do have some more. You're dying as much as I am to see what happens next."

He signaled the waiter for another glass, and when they lifted them in a toast, he whispered ominously, "Good luck."

"I'll consider myself properly warned." She smiled back.

It was too obvious a joke, everything he told her; but to be the center of his attention, however fanciful and outrageous, was dangerously flattering to her. How ludicrous that after confessing to her that he was the experienced playboy she had always suspected, she was now finding it harder than ever to believe it. But wasn't that the ploy? she warned herself, marveling once again at how the candlelight complimented his handsome face. The business she had been so eager to discuss could wait. It would surely remind him of his injured thoroughbred, and for the moment she didn't want anything to trouble that brow of his.

"Come, bring your glass. I want to show you something."

The edge of the patio overlooking the water was guarded by a sheet of glass, a windbreak, with a small

Take 4 Books
-and a Mystery Gift-
FREE

**And preview exciting new Silhouette Romance novels
every month — as soon as they're published!**

Silhouette Romance®

Yes...Get 4 Silhouette Romance novels (a $7.80 value) along with your Mystery Gift FREE

SLIP AWAY FOR AWHILE... Let Silhouette Romance draw you into a love-filled world of fascinating men and women. You'll find it's easy to close the door on the cares and concerns of everyday life as you lose yourself in the timeless drama of love, played out in exotic locations the world over.

EVERY BOOK AN ORIGINAL... Every Silhouette Romance is a full-length story, never before in print, superbly written to give you more of what you want from romance. Start with 4 brand new Silhouette Romance novels—yours free with the attached coupon. Along with your Mystery Gift, it's a $7.80 gift from us to you, with no obligation to buy anything now or ever.

YOUR FAVORITE AUTHORS... Silhouette Romance novels are created by the very best authors of romantic fiction. Let your favorite authors—such as Fern Michaels, Anne Hampson, Janet Daily, Nora Roberts, and many more—take you to a whole other world.

ROMANCE-FILLED READING... Each month you'll meet lively young heroines and share in their trials and triumphs...bold, virile men you'll find as fascinating as the heroines do...and colorful supporting characters you'll feel you've known forever. They're all in Silhouette Romance novels—and now you can share every one of the wonderful reading adventures they provide.

NO OBLIGATION... Each month we'll send you 6 brand-new Silhouette Romance novels a full two months *before* they are available in stores. Your books will be sent to you as soon as they are published, without obligation. If not enchanted, simply return them within 15 days and owe nothing. Or keep them, and pay just $1.95 each (a total of $11.70). And there's never an additional charge for shipping and handling.

SPECIAL EXTRAS FOR HOME SUBSCRIBERS ONLY... When you take advantage of this offer and become a home subscriber, we'll also send you the Silhouette Books Newsletter FREE with each book shipment. Every informative issue features news about upcoming titles, interviews with your favorite authors, even their favorite recipes.

So send in the postage-paid card today, and take your fantasies further than they've ever been. The trip will do you good!

CLIP AND MAIL COUPON TODAY!

NO POSTAGE
NECESSARY
IF MAILED
IN THE
UNITED STATES

BUSINESS REPLY CARD

FIRST CLASS PERMIT NO. 194 CLIFTON, N.J.

Postage will be paid by addressee

Silhouette Books
120 Brighton Road
P.O. BOX 5084
Clifton, NJ 07015-9956

door in the corner almost hidden by the foliage. He took her hand and led her under a trellis of vines and down a series of flagstone steps. It was alarmingly dark except for a small patch of moonlight in a clearing below. They were getting close to the water. She could hear the gentle lap of waves rustling pebbles on the shore.

"Is there no end to this place? From the road it looks so tiny . . . ."

He stopped in the clearing on a swath of lawn just big enough for the two of them. A small path led away and down another foot or two to a sandy strand of beach. He took her glass from her hand and held it to her lips for the last few drops, then flung it into the sea along with his.

"This is my private little haven away from the world," he said. "I built it myself. Laid every stone. Built the trellis and planted the vines. The owner is an old friend. He wanted to repay me for a favor I did him by offering me a partnership in the restaurant, but all I wanted was this. Some summer nights I even sleep down here."

The breeze off the water was gentle, but cool. He put his arms around her shoulders and hugged her to his chest to keep her warm.

"I never brought anyone here before," he said, looking down into her eyes.

"Not even one of those hundreds of fair damsels?" she said, almost in a whisper.

"Nary a one. Funny, huh? I sure am proud of this place and the work I did. You'd have to see it in the daylight to really appreciate it."

"This wouldn't be plan B, now would it, Mr. Malone?" she asked, daring herself to believe she was privileged to share a part of him that he had never shared with anyone else.

"Plan B?" He smiled. "I don't know. I never tried plan B before."

"Never had to?"

He shrugged.

"Then you don't know what's supposed to come next?" she whispered. She stood on the tips of her toes and kissed him softly on his cheek, just to stop him from saying something that threatened to dispel the moment.

"Not exactly," he said, surprised that she would kiss him. He searched her eyes for an explanation. "But if I were to hazard a guess, I'd say that this would be the perfect moment to . . ." His hands enveloped her waist, and he lifted her up and kissed her softly on the lips. ". . . to kiss you. But never having put the plan into operation, I'm open for suggestions. Any ideas?"

Her arms were around his neck, and she didn't dare look at him as her fingers tangled themselves into his hair.

"No ideas," she lied as she rested her cheek against his. The clean scent of his hair coupled with the smell of the sea, wedding the essence of him with the dangers and excitement of night. No thinking. They were beyond words. Words were deceptive and unreliable, and they masked what she already knew . . . what she could no longer refuse to admit. She loved him! She loved him more than anything she had ever loved. That realization brought a strange relief that sapped her strength and diminished the small will she had left to resist him. How could she love him? she wondered. She hardly knew him.

As he felt her relax, he reached over to cradle her into his arms. She rested her head against his shoulder and watched the aura of the moon behind his head sparkle through his hair.

"I've got enough ideas for the two of us," he whispered. "They're all so different now. I never felt this way about . . ." He looked at her and a thought wrinkled his brow, filling his eyes with a sad excitement. "I want you to know . . ." But he stopped himself. "Never mind. You'd never believe it anyway. I hardly believe it myself."

"Believe what?"

"Believe that . . . that I'm starving," he lied. "You must be, too. Let's eat."

"French, Italian or seafood?" she asked.

"No French. But great Italian and the best seafood on the entire North Shore."

"I want the seafood," she said, knowing that what he had wanted to tell her was something very personal and from the heart. That was reassuring.

"I knew it. It's what I ordered for you."

"You did? Without even asking me? How did you know I wanted seafood?"

"I just guessed." He stood her on a step, and she was taller than him by a few inches. Her hair brushed against his face as she leaned on his shoulders. He closed his eyes and breathed in the aroma.

"How come you always guess right?" she whispered.

"Luck."

"Luck, my foot. Experience."

"Experience? You give me more credit than I deserve."

"No, I don't," she said, pushing herself away from him. He put his hands on his hips and shook his head. "And don't look so innocent," she said. "Everything about you is so . . . so smooth. You make me feel like another notch in your belt."

"Forget the seafood!" he said, exasperated that the mood, so lovely just a moment ago, was now irrevocably destroyed. "You're getting a hamburger and French fries!"

"There you go again, telling me what to eat!" She moved backwards up to the next step.

"Come over here," he said softly.

"No!" She turned and started to run up the stairs. The light from the patio above was just enough to navigate through the tunnel beneath the vines. She could hear him running up behind her, and when he grabbed her at the top of the tunnel, just as she was about to open the glass door, she cried out. He turned her swiftly into his arms and smothered her cries with his lips. She struggled to free herself, but knew he wasn't going to let her go.

She gave up the fight and released herself into his arms, parting her lips to receive his kiss with all the resolve of a woman in love, with all the bittersweet agony of doubt that he could ever be truly hers. It didn't matter. Not now. Not as long as he held her in his warm embrace.

Chapter Seven

"Truce?" He relaxed his hold and kissed the tip of her nose.

"Truce."

He opened the door for her, and she stepped onto the patio and into the view of two couples seated at the tables. She realized at once that they had been watching them kiss, and she flushed with embarrassment.

"Oh, Garret," she whispered to him, feeling the urge to hide herself in his arms, "see what you've done?"

"Me?" He laughed, putting his arm around her shoulder and guiding her to their table. "If you hadn't run off like a little . . . a little . . ."

"A little what?"

"Truce, remember?"

"Your table is ready in the dining room, Mr.

Malone," the waiter informed him before they could sit down.

"Thank goodness," Adrianna sighed, glad to escape those strangers who made no effort whatsoever to conceal their enjoyment at her expense.

The table for two overlooked the water. The windows reflected the lavender light of the room but not strongly enough to hide the lights on the distant shore. The champagne reappeared, and the empty crystal goblets were filled with the sparkling drink. If love had colors, they would be amber, like wine, and lavender, like lace cloth, and blue, like his eyes that softly caressed her face and spoke with the wonder of silence what her soul was longing to hear. A moment in time, charmed forever by the breath of a wish.

The seafood was a delicate affair served in bite-sized tastes. Garret tirelessly explained what each one was and how it was prepared. Just the sound of his voice was enough to delight Adrianna. Could anything be more wonderful?

"They're all so scrumptious. I'll never remember what each one is," she said. He had ordered a steak for himself.

"You will. If you have them again. Next time, you'll have to try the veal."

Next time? Would there be a next time? She looked at her purse and thought of the check she was carrying to pay for Sarazen. She should mention it over coffee and get that business settled once and for all. But was tonight the proper time? He was so enthused with her. *Nothing must remind him of his ailing horse,* she told herself, remembering the anxiety in his face when he told her about it. There would be time enough later.

When the coffee was served, the waiter whispered something to him, and he slowly rose to his feet.

"Telephone call for me. The X rays are back." The

anxiety she'd tried to avoid was now evident in his face. He was expecting the worst, and he was gathering his thoughts to prepare himself.

"Good luck," she said, touching his hand as he walked past her.

She stirred her coffee and lost herself in the solitude of her apprehension. How she hated to see him so troubled. *Hope for the best and the best will come,* she told herself, looking out at the water.

A reflection in red filled the window. It was shaped by the cut glass into a work of modern art, a Picasso of angles. She studied it a moment before she realized it was alive, the image of a person standing at the table waiting for her to turn around.

"So, you're the business Garret had to attend to?" the woman dressed in red said, pulling her shoulders back to emphasize the remark. Anger seethed from her large black eyes, making her appear haughtily arrogant, a posture she wore as expertly as her clothes. She was extremely beautiful. A raven-haired sophisticate, tall and elegant.

"I beg your pardon?" Adrianna said, alarmed that she could be the object of the hatred in those eyes.

"Stop it! Don't play dumb. I don't like being the other woman, and I won't allow it. Do you hear?"

The room grew quiet as the diners around them noticed the possibility of a scene. A man hurriedly approached the woman from behind and tried to turn her around. She slapped his hands away and spoke to him without lifting her eyes from Adrianna.

"Do you understand it, George?" she said. George was embarrassed for her, but also for himself as he stood helplessly behind her, unable to take her from the room. "No, you wouldn't," she sneered contemptuously.

"Lydia, please," he said quietly. He glanced about

and saw that she was now the focus of attention of the entire room. "You're making a scene." His eyes were pleading.

"A scene? A scene?" Lydia intoned, stumbling against the table and quickly regaining her balance. "Me being seen with you, you wimp, is a scene," she said, turning her contempt away from Adrianna and aiming it solely at him.

Garret entered the room and was making his way towards them. It was obvious by his demeanor that the news he had received was serious, too serious for him to tolerate the unexpected petulance of this woman, whoever she was. He turned Lydia around so quickly that she almost tripped and fell. He held her by the wrists and glared menacingly into her eyes.

"Just what do you think you're doing?" he whispered between his teeth. Lydia tried to refocus her angry eyes, but they were no match for his.

"I'm sorry, Garret," George said. Lydia didn't try to speak. She knew the danger and the risk of crossing Garret Malone. "I could have had her home by now," George added, "but I can't start my car."

"Take mine," Garret said, releasing Lydia but fixing her with just the power of his eyes. He tossed George his car keys. "Take her home. Now."

"I don't want him to take me home," Lydia said, pouting and batting her long eyelashes in a pathetic attempt to regain her composure.

"I don't want to know what you want!" Garret hissed at her, ending whatever thoughts she had of appeasing him. He took both of them by the arm and led them towards the exit. When he returned to the table, the room hadn't quite settled. He took one look around that seemed to satisfy everyone's curiosity, and before he could sit they were once again anonymous and alone.

"I'm sorry for that . . . that . . . nonsense," he said, pushing his hands through his hair to rid himself of the incident. "Another hazard of the horse business. That was Lydia Worthington, the spoiled daughter of Sarazen's previous owner. I've barred her from the stable area as a nuisance, and she hasn't quite recovered."

"I'd say she's in love with you," Adrianna said, Lydia's dark eyes still flashing in her memory.

"Hardly. She's insulted that she can't control me, the way she manipulates all the other employees of her

father. To her, thoroughbreds are just a diversion, a frill for the super-rich. And I'm just another caretaker. It's all such a game to her. Her father buys and sells these animals without ever . . . touching them."

Or without being touched by them, she added, reading his thoughts. "How's the horse?" she said to change the subject, watching the sadness envelop him like a cloud, a sadness he had tried to guard himself against.

He touched her hand, and for a moment he was glad that she was there, that she was capable of understanding how he felt. "Real bad. I've got to destroy him."

"Oh, Garret!" The tears welled up in her eyes, and she wanted to reach out to him. "Why do you have to . . . ?" She stopped herself when he looked at her, surprised that she could ask that question, that she didn't know enough about him already to know that answer. She wished in one impetuous moment that Lydia were back, if just to divert his attention and rile up his anger enough to kill off the profound sadness in his eyes.

"I'll need a ride to the track. Do you mind?"

"Of course not. How soon do you want to leave?"

"As soon as you're ready."

"I'll never be ready for what you've got to do," she whispered. "Never."

He took a deep breath and stood up. "You're okay, Adrianna Adams." He smiled at her. "I hope we can do this again sometime."

Hope? Where was that self-confidence of his that she found so disturbing, that would tell her when he wanted to have dinner with her again? That maddening manner of his she would eagerly settle for in place of the sorrow that was quickly draining his strength.

He signed the check in the lobby and asked that it be added to his account.

"Everything was satisfactory, Mr. Malone?" the maître d' asked.

"Just great. My friend, here, loved the food. Our compliments to Andre."

"Thank you. We hope to see you again, Miss Adams," he said, with a slight nod of the head.

"You will. I hear the veal is superb," she said. "Book me a table for tomorrow night. The same table we had tonight."

The maître d' smiled and looked at Garret for his confirmation.

"Don't look at me." He smiled at him and then glanced at Adrianna. "The young lady must have a date."

"I do," she said. "I do."

He was content to let her drive, but she made some excuse about not knowing the road and said that she would feel safer if he took the wheel. It would keep him occupied, perhaps divert his attention a little from the terrible business he felt it was his duty to perform. The night air had cooled appreciably. He raised the roof of her car and locked it securely into place.

As he turned onto the road, she looked back at the

restaurant to fix it indelibly in her mind. Those few brief hours had been a happy dream. How quickly the world reclaimed them, as if that time were an aberration, that place a rare combination of everything that never should have been.

She studied his face in the dark light, and she could see the determination chiseled in his jaw. He was settled on his course of action, and there was nothing anyone could say or do to dissuade him.

"I had a wonderful time, Garret," she said.

"So did I. Too bad about this business. I'll make it up to you. And Lydia, busting in like that. Glad you didn't get the wrong idea."

"The wrong idea? What's the wrong idea? The woman is obviously in love with you. And she's strikingly beautiful."

"But you're more beautiful." He reached over and touched her knee, and the sensation sent a chill down her spine. "You have a date tomorrow night?"

"Why do you ask?"

"The reservation at Arpeggio's. I thought you were hell-bent on getting home with your horse?"

"What's one more day?"

He looked over at her. "Anyone I know?"

"Who?"

"Your date. Anyone I know?"

"Maybe. If not, you should. He's very tall and good-looking. And too stubborn for his own good. Loves to boss people around. Always has to have his own way."

"You like that about him?"

"What? That he's tall and good-looking?"

"No. That he always has to have his own way?"

"Not as much as I like the soft and tender side of him. It surfaces every once in a while when he least expects it."

"You like him?"

"Yeah. I like him."

"Does he care for you? I mean, does he really care for you?" He pulled the car to the side of the road, shut the engine off and turned towards her. "You shouldn't go out with him if you think he doesn't . . . really like you."

"I don't know. He has so many . . . friends. You know, fawning all over him. Insanely jealous when he stands them up to go out with me."

"A ladies' man? Bad choice. Dump him. He'll break your heart."

He already has. "I think you're right. I'll take your advice and . . . dump him."

She watched his gaze travel over her dress and felt her body was being caressed. The power of his eyes alone was enough to arouse her passion.

"When will you dump him? Over champagne, or later, after the dessert?"

"I haven't decided."

"What if—what if he refuses to be dumped?"

"I never thought of that."

"Think of it. He sounds like he's the type who doesn't take no for an answer. He may come after you. Do you want him to come after you?"

"I . . . I . . ."

He was nibbling on her earlobe, nuzzling his nose in the soft pocket behind her ear. His hand, which was pressed against her waist, slowly moved up and surrounded her breast.

"Do you want him to come after you? And make love to you?"

His mouth found hers open, inviting the swarming passion of his tongue to explore her desire, to know, by the sensuous appetite he aroused in her, the answer to that question.

"No . . . please." She took his hand in hers and kissed it tenderly. "Go. Start the car."

He kissed her forehead and then softly kissed her eyes till she held them shut in the spell of a dream.

"This date of yours . . . I bet you have him doing back flips over you."

"Not really." She smiled, not opening her eyes. "He's not that type."

"Oh? What does he do? I mean, how does he let you know that he thinks you're something very special? Something he's never experienced before? Someone he has the devil of a time trying to figure out. A real nut job, that he can't get out of his mind?"

"A nut job?!" Her eyes flew open, but he kissed her soundly on the lips and then started the engine before she could object. The business he had to attend to had suddenly overpowered his thoughts. He got the car into fifth gear, put his arm around her shoulder and pulled her close to him. She knew he was going to be okay; that he had himself in control and that she had nothing to fear. There was nothing to be afraid of. They drove in silence the rest of the way.

He stopped the car at the gate to the track and opened his door to get out.

"No, Garret. I want to be with you."

"This is no easy business. You'd better go home."

"No. I want to be here. Don't fight me on this."

He showed his pass to the night guard, drove past the gate and turned left. He parked in front of his office and shut off the lights. The street was completely dark except for the light coming out of one of the stalls. She could make out the shape of Floyd Hess leaning against a hitching rail. Why wasn't it his job to shoot the horse? It would be something he could do without a second thought.

They got out of the car, and Garret told her to wait

right where she was. He entered his office and re-emerged a few seconds later without his jacket. His sleeves were rolled up, and he had a revolver which he tried to hide from her by wrapping it in a towel.

"Wait in the office," he ordered. He walked slowly towards the stalls, and when she thought he was far enough away, she followed.

The men mumbled something to him as he approached the stall. As he opened the gate, Adrianna could see the horse lying on his side. A man with a stethoscope was kneeling next to the animal, and when Garret entered, he stood up. They conferred awhile, going over the X-ray photos. One by one, they held them up to the light and took turns pointing out some message they both agreed was unmistakably written on them.

Garret knelt down on one knee and gently patted the horse's cheek, reassuring the animal that he had nothing to fear. When he stood up, he escorted the man from the stall. *He must be a vet,* Adrianna thought. They shook hands again, and the vet walked slowly away into the darkened street. The other men who were standing around followed him.

In a few seconds she was the only witness left. Mesmerized by the drama unfolding before her, she stepped closer and held her breath. Garret was kneeling next to the animal's head and gently rubbing its face.

He leaned over and whispered something into the horse's ear, then hugged him tenderly, rocking that large head softly in his lap. He took a piece of sugar from his shirt pocket and held it against its nose till it nibbled it from his hand. When he eased the horse's head from his lap and rested it in the straw, Adrianna turned and ran away.

She sat on the couch in his office and waited for

what seemed like hours. A small desk lamp with a green glass shade barely lit the room. She never heard the shot. She didn't know it was over until she saw him standing in the doorway. A towel with the gun in it was under his arm. He walked over and sat down next to her.

"Are you okay?" he asked, taking her hands and studying her face. "You were crying. Don't be sad for him. It was painless. Instantaneous. There was nothing else to be done."

"I know. I was thinking . . . about you."

He smiled and slipped his arm around her shoulder. "Come. It's time you went home."

"What about you?"

"I'm staying here."

"Where? On this couch? I'll drive you home."

"No. I've got things to do."

He walked her to her car and held her in his arms a long time before kissing her good night.

"Please, Garret, take the flower from my hair."

He reached over and extracted the yellow daylily from her hair. She held out her hand, and he laid it softly in her palm, gently closing her fingers around it.

Chapter Eight

Marcie tore open the curtains, and the bedroom exploded into light.

"Child! Why didn't you get undressed?"

Adrianna had fallen asleep in her white sundress. She had meant to change and crawl in under the covers just a minute ago, or so it seemed—just when she finally gave up trying to figure out what Garret could have whispered to that horse. It must have been something profound. But what could be more profound than kindness—the simple heartfelt affection of one being reaching out to another?

Exhausted by the traumatic night, she experienced only now, in these first real moments of peace, the answer she had been searching for. It was as easy as love, as simple as a flower, as vital as the sun pouring life into a room, and just as wonderfully inexplicable.

"And what, may I ask, do we have here?" Marcie perched on the edge of the bed and touched Adrianna's clasped hands. "Oh, my," she said, smiling as her hands uncovered the flower. She brushed the hairs off Adrianna's forehead and then let her warm soft hand touch her cheek. "I hope that means you'll be staying awhile longer than you originally planned. Your father called last night. He wants to know when you're coming home. What are you going to tell him, child?"

"I don't know."

"Well, while you're making up your mind, I've got work for you to do. I need to do the grocery shopping today, and I need some pretty young miss to tell me what she wants to eat for dinner, for the next week at least. I also need that young miss to drive. Never did learn myself, and it's the chauffeur's day off. What do you say? It'll keep your mind off this," she said, lifting the wilted flower ceremoniously by the stem. "We need to find the right book to press this into. For now, we'll leave it on the nightstand under the lamp. The heat will help to dry it." Marcie put it on the stand and turned on the light. "And now, young lady, up and at 'em!"

A warm shower brought her body slowly back to life. The heat worked its healing powers into the muscles behind her neck, loosening the tension that was caused by lying on her back immobile for hours. And suddenly she remembered how totally helpless she had felt watching him in the stall. Why couldn't the vet have given the horse a lethal drug? Why had it been so important that he do it himself? He took full responsibility for the horse's life and . . . death. A lesser man, a man less committed, would have delegated that responsibility.

She loved that man with all her soul.

She wore her dark corduroy slacks that tapered around her ankles like jogging pants. How wonderful they felt against her skin. The matching jacket felt snug around her back and shoulders, accenting the bolero sleeves that buttoned at the wrist. Her jonquil-colored blouse had a gorgeous lacy front that complemented her light golden hair. The outfit was ideal for this in-between season, as the early spring tried so gallantly to unleash the world from the bonds of winter.

Another beautiful day, unexpected and exciting, a day meant for vacation and idle business; for shopping with Marcie, keeping her mind wonderfully occupied so her heart could be left alone in the sweet agony of thoughts of him. Touching the flower on the nightstand, she was with him in his arms, swaying on that patch of grass by the sea.

Marcie was as efficient as she was dictatorial. Equipped with her lists and ledger book, she directed Adrianna from markets on the North Shore to shops and delicatessens as far away as Brooklyn. She knew exactly what she wanted and, within a penny, the price of everything by the pound. Everything was wrapped, to be delivered "no later than tomorrow or I'll send it back," she always said, winking at Adrianna and shaking her head.

Every merchant knew her by name. She had been dealing with them for a century, she said. "They save stuff for me. And if I don't show up when they expect me, they get awfully put out. I love it," she laughed.

She had anecdotes about them all. With most, she bantered good-naturedly about their exorbitant prices and asked about their families and listened to their stories before waving farewell with an exasperated look that asked why she was so foolish as to continue to shop there. "They love that." They did. "I make them think I'm doing them a favor, and they make me think I'm robbing them blind." A game made all the more enjoyable, Adrianna suspected, because no one was fooling anyone.

It was a fascinating tour. Adrianna learned hundreds of things about food just listening to Marcie as she pointed out the telltale signs of fresh produce and well-cured meat.

"I saved the best for last, child," Marcie said, waving a finger for Adrianna to turn right at the next corner. They were somewhere in Brooklyn on a narrow street, inching along the bottom of a canyon of high-rise apartments. It was a one-way street with cars parked on either side.

"We should have taken the sports car, Marcie. I'll never find a parking space large enough for this . . . this barge."

"We need it, dear. Sal doesn't deliver. Turn here. Halfway down the block there's an alley. There it is. Park it there."

The sidewalks were crowded on both sides with shoppers, neighborhood people shopping in the small stores that lined the sidewalks one after the other.

Adrianna pulled into the alley and turned off the engine. The car was so tightly wedged between the brick walls, she wondered if she would ever be able to back it out without tearing off the fenders. A wooden door in the brick wall was half open, and from it emanated the most heavenly scents of fresh-baked bread.

Marcie led the way. Once inside the door, they were in the middle of a baker's kitchen, waiting for a heavyset middle-aged man, dusted white with flour and powdered sugar, to look up from the pile of dough he was strangling and beating into shape.

"Marcie!" he yelled when he saw her. He pinched

off a piece of dough and brought it over to her to taste. "What do you think? Too much salt?"

"Perfect, Sal, as always. This is Alex's niece, Adrianna. Adrianna, this is Sal. I went to school with his father. And this"—she swept her arm around the kitchen—"is the best bakery on the entire East Coast of the United States."

The bakery was very small. In the front were a few tables for customers to drink coffee, take in the aromas and sample the confectionery delights.

"I buy all my bread and cakes and rolls and donuts from Sal. Half of it is for Alex's neighbors. He tells them I bake it all myself. Don't ever tell them the truth," she said with a wink.

A young girl poured them coffee, and Marcie recommended the specialty of the house, chocolate éclairs so large and soft they had to be eaten with a fork.

"What a marvelous day I've had," Adrianna said, tasting her éclair.

"Shopping? I should think you'd have a hundred things you'd much rather be doing than sitting in a little bakery in the heart of Brooklyn with a cantankerous old biddy like me."

"You taught me so much today. I'll never remember it all."

"Don't try. Everything you ever need to know, you will know. So," she said, taking a sip of coffee and settling her elbows for a long chat, "tell me all about him."

It was late afternoon when she turned the station wagon onto the gravel drive of the estate. She had told Marcie everything, more than she probably should have. Maybe it was the way Marcie had shared so much of her life with her, or the proud way Marcie had looked when she introduced her to her shopkeepers, as if she were her daughter.

"And the horse?" she asked when Adrianna shut off the engine. "You closed the deal for the horse?"

"No . . . I was going to mention it to him, but with Lydia barging in like that, and then his having to go back to the track . . . it just wasn't the right time."

"Well, there's time enough for all that. Go call your father, and I'll have this car unloaded. Are you eating here tonight, or do you have another date?"

"I'm not sure. We . . . barely discussed it."

"Call him up and invite him over here."

"I couldn't."

"Why not? I could make steaks. He sounds like a steak man to me."

It wasn't the idea that she couldn't invite him, it was that she had never before called a man for a date. She had been bold enough last night to make reservations at Arpeggio's. But not bold enough to tell him directly that her date for the evening was to be him. What if he misunderstood? What if he really thought she had a date with someone else?

"I'll see, Marcie," she said, no longer sure of anything.

She went to her room and dialed the number of her home.

"Dad? It's me. How are you?"

"Fine. And how are you?"

"Great, Dad. The horse is even better than I thought he would be. How are things going?"

"The weather has been perfect up here. Just what I needed to finish planting the vines. It's going to be a great year. I just know it. I called last night and Marcie said you had a date. What's the story?"

"No story. Trying to close the deal for the horse."

"You sound like you're keeping something from me. What is it?"

"You know I can't keep anything from you—for very long, anyway."

"Got that heater working in the barn. When do you think you'll be trailering that thoroughbred up here?"

"I was planning on leaving last night. Maybe tomorrow. Maybe . . . a little later than that. I just don't know right now. I'll let you know."

"Sweetheart?"

"What, Dad?"

"There's no rush. Remember that. You take your time. Take all summer if you have to. I'd much rather see you down there at Alex's than wasting your time up here. You only get in the way, anyway."

"I do not. Who'd ruin your coffee and burn your steaks into little charcoal briquets if it weren't for me?"

"That's what I mean." He laughed. "Since you left, I discovered real food again."

"What? I thought you loved my cooking?!" She laughed, remembering him at the kitchen table trying to cut her flapjacks with a knife.

"Marcie is a real cook. Have you seen her use a fire extinguisher yet?"

"One little accident and you'll never let me live it down!" She was laughing so hard she fell back on the bed. Two years ago, she had left a pound of bacon sizzling on the stove to go and make one little phone call. An hour later, smoke was billowing through the house. When her father had come running in from the barn, he'd found her in the kitchen with a fire extinguisher in her hand and her face black with soot. In minutes he had her doubled over, laughing at herself and her innovative culinary techniques.

"I promised the boys at the fire station I'd let them know when you'll be back," he teased.

"You're cruel and heartless. See if I ever cook for you again."

"Promises, promises," he chortled amiably. "You'll be doing me a favor if you stay long enough to get a few hints from Marcie. Hey, it can't hurt."

"That's it!" she teased. "I'm running away from home. You'll never see me again as long as you live!"

"I miss you, sweetheart. But seriously, there's no rush."

"I love you, you old . . . troublemaker."

"I love you. Give a hoot and a holler if you need anything, you hear?"

"Bye, Daddy."

"Bye, baby."

She waited a long time for the ghost of that laughing, lovable man to leave before she called information for the number of the office of Worthington Stables. She would say nothing about last night. Just ask about Sarazen and when it would be most convenient to sign over the papers.

She listened to her heartbeat between the rings of the phone. Any second and his voice would be so close to her ear . . . she imagined him nibbling her earlobe. The thought sent a chill tingling down her spine.

"Worthington Stables." She recognized the voice of Floyd Hess. What was he doing in Garret's office?

"Mr. Malone, please."

"Mr. Malone ain't here."

She pictured the grizzled little man behind Garret's desk, his feet up and a cigar stub wedged in the corner of his mouth.

"Do you know when he'll be back?"

"No."

She didn't expect he would know anything about Garret's whereabouts. She waited a second for an explanation, and when it didn't come, she knew he was being intentionally rude. *Maybe he's guessed it's me,* she thought. "Well, if I hold, will you go and look for him?" Her anger was quickly rising to the boiling point.

"He ain't here, lady," he snarled and slammed the phone down.

She redialed the number, but before it could ring, she hung up. There was no sense getting into an argument with him. If Garret wasn't there, Hess was in charge. And that meant Sarazen was under his care. Not that Floyd Hess would be vindictive enough to go out of his way to abuse the animal, but why take chances? The sooner she had Sarazen moved to her uncle's stalls, the better. It was too late to go down to the track. By the time she got there, the stalls would be locked. And even if they weren't, if Garret wasn't there, she couldn't take Sarazen. She wouldn't go behind his back.

She had the reservation at Arpeggio's, and she could go there alone. He could be down at the water at his idyllic little haven away from the world. Or he could be in the dining room with a date. Why wouldn't he have another date? He certainly didn't commit himself to taking her to dinner. She should have been more direct.

It was hopeless. But she couldn't help imagining the possibilities or trying to relive last night with the cold objectivity of a disinterested observer. Impossible. That he was infatuated with her when his passions were aroused was quite clear. Yet it was impossible for her to imagine that he didn't feel something more meaningful than desire.

She offered to help in the kitchen, but Marcie was busy with her ledger books, making entries for all the supplies she'd ordered.

"Do you have a date, child?"

"I don't know."

"If not, it'll be just the two of us. I'll show you how to make my favorite stew."

"Has my father been talking to you?"

Her eyes grew large and she smiled. "Why, child," she laughed, "I haven't the faintest idea what you're talking about."

"If I know him, he gave you a list of his favorite dishes and implored you to see what you could do to enhance the cooking skills of his untalented daughter."

"Not true." She grinned. "Well, not entirely true."

"I knew it. Okay. What's first? Peeling? Dicing? Slicing? Paring? I'm ready."

"That's the spirit. I'll be with you in a minute. You could do me a favor and go out to the flower garden and see what bloomed. Cut a bunch to fill a vase. You know how your uncle just loves fresh flowers in the house."

The garden was behind the gazebo and a wall of Italian cypress trees. In midsummer, the colors would be bright enough to hurt her eyes. But in early spring, the grounds were sparse. The long-stemmed daffodils offered the best pickings. She smelled each one before stripping the stem and placing the flower in a large vase.

The sun was setting behind the house. Before too long, she would be in its shadow. But she took her time selecting the flowers and experimenting with the arrangement as she added each one to the collection. *No rush,* she could hear her father say. That memory

gave her permission to allow the peace she had
experienced that afternoon to return, and with it, the
joy of anticipation. It was almost too consuming, as
if . . . as if were she to turn around, she would see
Garret standing there watching her, studying her face
to pick out the feature he wanted to kiss first.

She stood up, and the feeling was now more intense
than she had ever felt it. There, on the pathway
behind the trees, was a figure, a man walking towards
the garden. The vase slipped from her hands when he
saw her and started running towards her, freeing her
arms to open wide and wrap so wonderfully around
him.

He swept her up and spun her around in his arms
and held her so tightly she could barely breathe.
"Where have you been all day?" he whispered into
her ear. "I called you a dozen times."

He kissed her cheek and then her eyes and then her
nose, and then her lips, until her heart was beating
with joy. He looked strong again. The sadness had left
him unscathed, and she once again admired that
confident masculinity that ignited his eyes.

"We have a date tonight at Arpeggio's. Eight
o'clock," she said. "If we hurry, we can catch the
sunset down by the water."

"What happened?" he teased. "Your date stand
you up?"

"What?"

"I thought you had a date for tonight."

"Oh, yes," she said, taking the hint and playing
along. "As a matter of fact, he did. I guess it'll just
have to be you." She reached up and grabbed the hair
behind his head in both hands.

"Oh, really? I don't play second fiddle to anyone.
It's me and no one else, or . . ."

"Or what?"

"I'm thinking . . . of something hideous, like locking you in a closet."

"You're sounding more and more like my father every time I see you."

"Is that good or bad?"

"He's a real special guy. You would like him," she said, kissing him softly on the lips.

"I'd just as soon not have him know my intentions to ravish his daughter."

"Oh, ravish, is it? Is that part of plan B? Or are you going to try another tactic altogether?"

"Yes, something entirely different. Plan C." He held her tightly and kissed her forehead.

"How does that one go? Or is it a surprise?"

"I have no idea at all. Plan C isn't a plan at all. It's something I've never allowed myself to do before."

"What's that?"

"Plan nothing at all. Let whatever happens . . . happen."

He nuzzled his nose into her neck and the sharp stubble of his beard scratched her cheek, provoking a desire to touch him, to feel him closer, much closer to her. How infuriating, the madness of imagining him making love to her. She knew she would give herself to him and never know if he truly loved her. How unfair that her body should demand sweet revenge for her hesitancy.

"Come, we'll walk back to the house." He picked up the vase and handed it to her and took a step backwards to get a better look at her. She put her arm in his and leaned against him as they slowly walked through the garden.

He wore a faded tan denim shirt with the sleeves rolled up to the elbows. It contoured his upper body like a handmade garment. She rubbed her cheek against the fabric and wondered how anything so ordinary could be transformed into something so rich and beautiful. He could work all day in a shirt like that and still look neat and trim.

"I have a house out in the Hamptons. I'd like to take you out there someday. It's beautiful. Three stories with a garden behind it, something like this but not as large."

"And there's no one living in it? No wife or children?"

"Let me think. No. No wife and no children."

"Sounds dangerous. You'd have me trapped out there all alone. How would I ever defend myself?"

"Alone? I have a grandmother as fidgety and cantankerous as a nest of hornets. She would look after you like a hen over her chicks."

"Sounds like you've given her plenty of reasons to be so protective of your . . . friends."

"Sounds like you're fishing around to find out how often I bring one of my . . . friends . . . home to meet the folks."

"You're right, it does sound like that. Well? How often?"

He stopped and put his hands on her shoulders and looked at her as he decided on his answer. "You're just going to have to wait and ask her yourself."

"Well, if that's your answer," she said, taking his arm again in hers, "then I'll just have to wait and ask her."

"Good. But she may lie to you. Tell you what she thinks you want to hear."

"And what do you suppose," she asked, "she'll think I would want to hear?"

"Something like, 'How nice of Garret to bring you out to meet me,' and 'How worried I was that he would never meet a nice girl like you and settle down.'"

"And how would I know if she's lying to me?"

"Watch her eyes. I'll be standing behind you and signaling to her."

"What?"

He laughed, took his arm away from her and ran ahead. "I'll be mouthing something like, 'Tell her that you think I must be in love with her.'"

She lifted the vase as if to throw it and chased after him. He raised his hands to protect his head and laughed as he ran across the lawn.

"You're impossible!" she screamed.

"And then I'll mouth something like, 'Tell her that I have never brought anybody home before and that this must be pretty serious!'" He was running backwards just out of her reach. He didn't see the stone bench behind him. He tripped over it and fell to the lawn, chuckling to himself when she caught him. She sat on his chest and he allowed her to pin his arms over his head. His laughter was so infectious, she found it extremely difficult not to join in.

"Do you always have your grandmother do your lying for you?"

"I wouldn't be lying," he said, rolling her over onto the lawn and pinning her arms. "I wouldn't be lying."

He kissed her so tenderly, she thought the world had stopped and everything in it was holding its breath. Did he know what he had said?

"Yoo-hoo!" Marcie called. She was standing in the kitchen door with her hands on her hips. "Is everything okay?" she teased. "I saw you giving mouth-to-mouth resuscitation, and I thought you might need an oxygen bottle or something. No?"

"No, Marcie," Adrianna said, getting up on her elbow. And to Garret she added in a whisper, "Everything here is just fine."

"Just fine indeed," he whispered back.

He pulled her up to her feet, and they both gathered the flowers that were strewn over the lawn. She led him into the kitchen and waited for Marcie to look up from her books.

"Marcie, this is Garret, the gentleman I've been telling you about."

"I know, we met at the door," she said amiably. "You're just in time for Adrianna's first cooking lesson."

"Marcie? This is hardly the time to . . ."

"You like stew, Garret? Good hearty stew with lots of onions and chunks of sirloin?"

"I love it," he said.

"I thought so. Grab an apron. You can peel the potatoes."

"Marcie!"

"Oh, hush. With all that, er . . . resuscitation going on, I should think you'd both be starving to death."

"We have a date, Marcie, and . . ."

"I'm going to have to take a rain check on that stew," Garret said to Marcie.

"See?" Adrianna added. "I think it's awfully forward of you to put a guest to work in the kitchen."

"Not at all," he contradicted her. "There is nothing I would rather do more than to stay and eat with you. I just came over to say good-bye."

"Good-bye?" Adrianna's heart sank into her stomach, and again the vase slipped from her hands. This time it shattered into a hundred little pieces.

Chapter Nine

"Go, the both of you," Marcie said. "I'll clean up this mess. Nice meeting you, Garret."

"Nice meeting you, too," he said, nodding his head at Adrianna to see him to the door.

"Where are you going?" she said when they reached the foyer.

"Business trip. There's a sale of two-year-old thoroughbreds in Kentucky tomorrow morning. I have to fly out tonight."

"This is awfully sudden, isn't it?"

"It wasn't planned, if that's what you mean. Neither was Fargo's accident. I need a replacement for him. It's what I do for a living, remember?"

"When will you be back?" She touched his hand and just as suddenly let it go.

"No telling. A few days. A week."

"What about . . . Sarazen?"

"What about him?"

"We never closed the deal for him."

"I know." He raked his hand through his hair and sighed. "I'd appreciate it if you'd hold off on that awhile longer. When I get back, we'll settle up and make it all legal."

She watched his eyes cloud with apprehension and sensed he was holding something back. "When I saw you with Sarazen yesterday, how fond you are of him and he of you, I wondered how on earth you ever had the heart to enter him in that claiming race. It doesn't make sense, Garret. Why?"

"Why? Because I didn't enter him in that race. I was away. I never would have allowed it had I been there to stop it."

"And now you're trying to stop me?"

"No, that's not it. If I turn him over to you now, you'll be gone by the time I get back. I'll never see you again. I don't want that to happen."

"I won't be gone. I'll stay."

"No. Not now. Try to understand."

"I could just as easily go to your office and sign those papers and pay the claiming price without you."

"You can't. I'll have the papers with me."

"You're stalling, and you're not telling me the entire truth," she quipped, noting that he wasn't used to being talked to like that. He set his jaw and narrowed his eyes into a threatening stare.

"I told you all I'm going to tell you right now. We'll talk about it when I get back."

"We'll talk about it right now," she said, leaning back against the door.

"You are something else," he said, shaking his head. "You accuse me of bossing people around! I said all I'm going to say about Sarazen."

"He's my horse, Garret. I'll get him. And you can't

sweet-talk your way out of it." It was a cruel thing to say, something she didn't really believe. Or did she? Why, when they met for the first time, did he hide the fact that he was Sarazen's trainer? That he knew nothing about horse racing when he picked the loser in the next race? That it was all a tragic mistake and he wanted the horse back, even if it meant he would have to sweet-talk the new owner into . . . ?

"Don't press it, little lady," he said. "He's your horse when I turn him over to you and not a moment before. You have your claim. Be satisfied with that. Your legal right to him begins when I give him up. And I'm not ready to do that right now."

"You can't just hold me up while you go off to Kentucky. I have a business to get started, and I'm anxious to get on with it."

"I know," he said, conceding the point and touching her shoulder. "I'm asking you as a friend to trust me. Just a few more days."

"You said a week."

"It won't be a week. I promise." He took her in his arms and hugged her tenderly. "You're so beautiful when you're angry. I couldn't bear to stay away from you for long."

"You make me angry."

"Good," he said, softly kissing her lips. "I'll be back before you realize I'm gone. In the meantime, you can learn how to make a good stew."

"Why? So I can cook it for you?"

"It's important. A woman should know how to please a man."

"Oh? I think a man should know how to please a woman."

"This man does."

If there was anything about him she could be positive of, it was that.

She waited until his car disappeared behind the stone wall at the road before she returned to the kitchen. Marcie was back at her books, pretending nothing had happened to warrant any concern from her.

"Men!" Adrianna said, grabbing an apron off the back of a chair. "What's so secretive about a good stew?"

It was still dark at five o'clock in the morning. The sky, barely visible, was overcast, laden with moisture that hung close to the ground. It thickened the morning air with a chilling mist. She had to turn her windshield wipers on twice, but not a drop had dampened the road, she noted as she fumbled in her purse for her track pass. The guard waved her through. He might have remembered her from yesterday. More likely, he remembered her car.

She parked under the trees. Sound traveled well in damp air. At this hour the stables were alive with noise. Hooves clopping, horses snorting out stale air from their lungs, cold leather creaking as it stretched under the weight of riders. A rustle of activity invisible from under the trees where she listened to it grow, like approaching cavalry making its way slowly through a forest.

She unlocked the trunk, kicked off her shoes and threw them in. Extracting her long black leather riding boots, she sat on the bumper to put them on. Her jeans were stirruped around the arches of her feet to hold them down as she pulled the leather over them and clinched the buckle at the top of her calves. Adrianna felt better with her boots on, more convinced that she had every right to do what she had come down here to do. She tucked her riding gloves in the back pockets of her jeans and locked her purse in the trunk.

"Sarazen, I hope I'm not too late," she whispered to herself as she walked down the street towards Worthington Stables. The street was busy with horses and men. The stalls were open and Sarazen was there, sniffing the activity, anxiously waiting his turn to get out for the morning run.

The riders were exercise boys whose sole job at the track was to exercise the horses they were assigned, to ride them in the way prescribed by the trainer. They were highly skilled, every bit the riders jockeys were, and most, if not all, had aspirations of riding in a real race one day. Some would never get the chance because of their size and weight, or because they lacked the instinct to get a horse to do exactly what it had to do to win, or because they simply didn't have the hand and arm strength to control a horse and conserve its energy for the burst at the top of the stretch.

Stable boys helped them with the saddling and teamed up when necessary to hold a horse impatient for his run. The horses coming back from the track were shrouded in steam as the heat pouring out of them vaporized in the cool air. They had to be walked to cool down and then rubbed and groomed and fed and watered. And all of these activities were going on simultaneously, each horse in a different cycle of its daily regimen.

Sarazen hadn't been run, she could tell just by looking at him. She wanted to run him, and she was preparing herself for any obstacle that would prevent her from doing so. The light in Garret's office was on, and Floyd Hess was probably in there. No need to disturb him. A rider carrying a saddle and bridle was approaching Sarazen's stall.

"Hi. You going to run him?" Adrianna said, touching his shoulder just before he opened the stall.

"Yes, ma'am," he said, turning toward her. "Last horse for today." He was short and slight of build. He had a round young boy's face with large, excitable eyes.

"How hard are you going to push him?"

"Not hard. He's been claimed. He ain't racing for us anymore."

"I know. I claimed him."

"You did? Hey, congratulations. You sure got yourself one fine horse."

"How do you know?" she said, glad he was friendly enough to open up to her. "He never won a race."

"Aw, you just know. This horse will do anything I tell him to. I can pace him in a quarter mile and count his strides, and he'd give me the same count for a mile and a half. It's unbelievable he never won. They ain't riding him right."

"That's what I think, too," she said. "My name is Adrianna Adams. What's yours?"

"Junior."

"Will you let me run him for you?"

"Oh, wow. I don't know. Mr. Malone will have my hide."

"Mr. Malone is in Kentucky."

"You know anything about riding?"

"Yeah." She smiled at him as he looked her up and down, trying to assess her riding ability. She took her gloves out of her back pocket and put them on.

"And you say you're the new owner?"

"Yes, Junior, I am."

"It's your horse. I hope you know what you're doing. Want me to saddle him for you?"

He worked quickly and efficiently. He had a good, firm sense about what he was doing. Within minutes he had Sarazen out in the street, trying to hold him still long enough to give Adrianna a leg up.

"When I get you up there, ma'am, don't go charging off. I'll walk-lead you-all down to the rail and show you where to run him. Okay?"

"You're the boss, Junior."

He gave her a lift into the saddle, and he helped her to readjust the length of the stirrups. He gave his instructions over his shoulder as he led them down the street.

"When you're running, get up over his shoulders and keep your head down. Talk to him. Encourage him. He'll listen, too. A slow gallop halfway around. At the five-furlong pole, let him go and just hang on. When you get back to the pole, slow him down for two or three furlongs and then let him go again for about a mile. No more than that. Got that?"

"I got it."

When they reached the entrance to the track, he handed her his helmet and told her to buckle it up tight. "Leave the goggles up. This is no race. And don't get close to any other horse to get mud thrown on you-all. Good luck. Stay off the rail."

"Junior?"

"Yeah?"

"Thanks."

"I'll wait right here and keep an eye on you. If I see anything wrong, I'll signal you to come in. And you come in, you hear?"

Sarazen dug into the dirt and bobbed his head as he pranced slowly out onto the track. The grandstand in the distance was just a darker shadow in the clouds. She nudged him in the ribs with her heels and leaned forward as he worked his powerful body up to an easy gait. His lungs devoured the air, stowing it like fuel and shooting back spent bolts of steam from his nostrils. Take it easy. Lubricate the muscles, raise the temperature, stoke up the heart and get it to pound, to energize this magnificent being to do what nature intended it to do better than any creature on earth. Run!

At the five-furlong pole, he was ready. She nudged him again and let out the reins to free his head and neck, to stretch out the stride and build up his speed. The faster he got, the smoother he ran, the easier to set her rhythm with his and keep up close to his ear.

"Go! Dig 'em in! Burn 'em up!"

He accelerated into the darkness, engulfing Adrianna in an eerie stillness, a gap between thought and reality where the only sound left on earth was her heart beating with his.

Past the finish line, then pole one, pole two, and no signs of tiring. She knew he would give everything he had and more if she let him. Pole five was coming up, and she pulled back to slow him down. He fought her off. She pulled harder, and still he resisted, trying to keep his nose up into the wind.

"Whoa. Whoa. Easy, boy. Easy."

Past the pole and he relented, letting her pull his head back to break his concentration.

"That a boy. Slow it down. I'll let you go again in a few minutes. Nice and easy now."

She forgot about Junior. She didn't dare turn around now. She let Sarazen go again, and this time when they passed the front of the grandstand, she heard the imaginary crowd cheering him on to the win. "It'll happen, Sarazen," she said into his ear. "It'll happen."

Junior was sitting on the rail, waiting for them. She had Sarazen back down into an easy gait as they approached him.

"Looking real good," he yelled to her. "One more

time around. Halfway, cut the pace in half and let him cool down."

She did exactly what she was told. As they finished the last circuit, Adrianna stood in the stirrups and hunched over Sarazen's ear. He'd had enough for the moment, but she could still sense the reserve of energy untapped in his body. She had never ridden a horse that fast in her life. Her face was tingling from the wind. She brought him down to a walk, and the steam pouring out of him followed them like a cloud.

"How'd we do?" Adrianna yelled as Junior took hold of the bridle.

"Not bad. You looked good out there, for a . . ."

"For a woman?"

"Yeah, for a woman. You weren't holding your hands in the right place, and your rear was too high. With a little coaching, you could be real good."

"I'll remember that, Junior. Maybe I can talk you into giving me lessons."

She dismounted, and together they walked Sarazen back towards the stalls. The sky had brightened considerably. The light was sufficient now to erase the sharp halos around the streetlamps. Junior gave her some pointers about her technique that she had never thought about, and she listened intently.

They took the long way to give Sarazen sufficient time to cool down slowly. When they did get back to the stalls, most of the activities of the morning had ceased. A few stable boys were left mucking out stalls. The riders and grooms were gone.

Junior put Sarazen in his stall and took off the bridle and saddle. "I'd stay to groom and water him, ma'am, but I've got to get going or I'll be late for work. Can't make enough money here to make ends meet."

"I guess none of you riders can. Have you thought

about being a jockey? You seem to be the right size."
He couldn't have been more than an inch taller than
she was, and he looked about the same age.

"Every exercise boy wants to be a jockey. I apply
for my license in a week."

"Good luck. If I race Sarazen, I sure would like you
to ride him," she said.

"I'll race him like he's never been raced before," he
said. The determination in his eyes alone convinced
her that he would do exactly that. "When are you
going to move him? Where are your stalls, anyway? I
never heard of you before, and I know all the owners
at this track."

"My uncle technically has the claim. Alex Trent."

"Yeah, Trent. He's just a few streets up that-a-
way."

"I don't know exactly when I'll be moving him.
Haven't signed the papers and paid for him yet. But
soon. Look for us there if you see Sarazen gone."

"That's a promise. You know how to groom a
horse?" he asked. She smiled and nodded. "The feed
is in the locker at the end of the stalls. Better check
with the trainer and find out how much."

She took her gloves off and held out her hand to
him. "You've been very helpful. I want to thank you
for all you've done."

He took her hand and smiled. "Don't thank me. If I
ever get to race him, that's all the thanks I want."

Adrianna worked slowly and methodically, taking
the opportunity to study every inch of Sarazen as she
carefully brushed his body back to its vibrant sheen.
A stable boy had given her a stool and offered to look
for Sarazen's feed chart. He found it, mixed the
required amounts for her and offered to hitch up the
feed bag around the horse's head.

She had no idea what time it was when she was

finally satisfied that all that had to be done was properly taken care of. The sky was solidly overcast and as bright as it was going to get. It was impossible to tell how high the sun was or even in what direction to look for it.

Walking back to her car, she finally allowed the exhaustion creeping into her bones to envelop her. It was a good, tired feeling; a respite from a workout that promised a greater sense of energy and well-being after a nice long break with a hot cup of coffee. And with a couple pieces of toast. And maybe an egg. Or a waffle. Anything. She was starved, and she didn't want to wait till she got back to the estate. All she could think of was how heavenly a nice breakfast was going to taste.

Floyd Hess was standing on the office porch, lighting up a new cigar with a wooden match.

"Come to visit your horse?" he said, puffing out a cloud of smoke and tossing the match into the street.

She didn't have to answer him; his intonation was sarcastic. But the knowledge that Sarazen would be under his care while Garret was away cautioned her not to snub him. The anger she had felt when he said Sarazen needed a good clout was still inside her.

"My uncle's horse. Alex Trent. He holds the claiming rights."

"Do tell? Well, I wouldn't be too sure about that. Garret has other ideas about letting him go." He took a deep drag and let the smoke trail slowly out of his pursed lips.

"I know all about Mr. Malone's ideas. I know it wasn't his idea to enter him in that race. There's nothing he can do about it now."

"Nothing? Maybe."

"What do you mean by that?"

"He could file a protest with the racing commissioner. Tie this whole thing up for months in litigation. There's a lot he can do."

"He wouldn't do that," she said, wishing she could say something that would wipe the smirk off his face. "When he gets back from Kentucky, this whole thing will be . . . straightened out."

"Kentucky? He told you he was going to Kentucky?" He held the cigar in his teeth and grinned. "I just saw him a moment ago at the cafeteria, talking with someone who looked real official."

"You did?"

He laughed and shook his head, enjoying the victory of having proven what he had suspected all along: that she was naive and knew nothing whatsoever about the thoroughbred-racing business.

"Sure did." He smiled. "I wouldn't bet on your chances of ever getting that horse, lady, if you can follow my drift."

"I follow your drift. Where's the cafeteria?"

"Make a right at the end of the street."

"Thanks. You're a real help," she said, trying as hard as she could to leave him with something to think about. "I'll be sure to tell Mr. Malone of your concern. That you sent me to talk to him about Sarazen. I bet he'll appreciate knowing that you're looking out for his best interests and all. If you can follow my drift?" She sent that message square into his eyes before smiling and turning away.

Turning right at the corner, she saw what she presumed was the cafeteria way off in the distance. She could barely make out the blue color of Garret's ca parked in front. Why had he lied to her? The thought drained her emotionally, leaving her weak and exhausted. That he would go behind her back to keep Sarazen was a devastating blow, a crippling punch at the foundation of their relationship. It was more than disappointment she felt, seeing herself in his arms, the reason for the spark in his eyes. That he could consciously deceive her meant that all that she had experienced with him was a mirage, an all too eager suspension of the cold, hard facts because of something she naively felt, childishly assumed since she had never fallen in love with any other man in her life. She leaned against the building to catch her breath as if she had been running for a long, long time in a dream from which she'd suddenly awoken. How could she have been so stupid? The sadness that consumed her almost took her legs out from under her.

The more the tears streamed down her face, the more her strength returned. Within the central core of her emptiness, a slow, deep breath fanned a glowing ember of anger. If all of this was always just the horse and nothing more, then so be it. She'd confront him with it now, in front of the racing official, and demand her legal right to Sarazen. *It all could have been so different,* she thought, but she saw at once the fallacy in that hopeless belief.

She walked back to her car to get her purse and the check she had been carrying with her for two days. The motion of her body set her resolve as she walked briskly toward the cafeteria. *I came to New York to get this horse and nothing more,* she reminded herself. By the time she reached the door to the cafeteria, she had rehearsed what she wanted to say and had committed it to memory.

Garret was in a booth against the far wall. He was wearing a white shirt and a tie that was pulled below his open collar. His sleeves were rolled up over his wrists, and his jacket was lying over the back of the booth next to him. The man sitting across from him was dressed in a three-piece business suit. The cafeteria was just a small coffee shop, crowded with track personnel. The only other woman in the place was a waitress carrying a tray of food to a table full of boisterous, laughing men. Garret was too absorbed in conversation to notice Adrianna as she walked quickly across the room.

She had the check in her hand. As he looked up and recognized her, she dropped it on the table in front of him.

"You have what I want. And I want it now!" Her anger deafened her to the sudden stillness that blanketed the room. Everyone was watching them, cocking their ears to get a handle on what it was she wanted that Garret had.

"Adrianna? What are you doing here?"

"I've come to get what's rightfully mine! There's the six thousand dollars, and not one penny more!"

"This is hardly the time . . ."

"I've waited long enough!" What little noise remained in the room was now completely extinguished as the crowd's attention focused on them. "Since you're not going to Kentucky, like you told me you were, I see no reason why we can't settle up now!"

Garret noticed the room was now waiting for him to answer. Being put on the spot was not something that was going to embarrass him, and he moved over for her to sit down next to him.

"Sit down."

"No more stalling. No more sweet talk. You are not going to talk your way out of this."

The man sitting across from Garret stirred nervously. He cleared his throat and waited with the rest of the room for Garret's reply.

Garret stared up at her for a long moment, searching her eyes for an explanation, the real reason for her indignation and anger. Whatever it was he found embittered him as he thought through the answer he now felt compelled to give. He grabbed her hand and forcefully shoved the check into it.

"A hundred times this amount wouldn't be enough."

"I agree. But that's your mistake."

"My mistake was not catching onto your scam and falling for your . . . your little masquerade." He whispered with such hatred in his voice, she almost turned to make sure he was talking to her and not to someone else standing behind her. The customers hadn't heard him, so they quickly gave up eavesdropping and regained their normal level of noise.

"I think I'd better be going," the man in the three-piece suit said as he stood up. They were no longer the focus of attention, and he took the opportunity to make his getaway. Garret pointed his finger at Adrianna and then jabbed it towards the seat vacated by the man, ordering her to sit down.

She did, and she waited for the man to say his good-byes. He touched Garret's shoulder and shook his head disbelievingly.

"I always knew you had a way with the ladies, Garret, but this . . . this desperation. I never would have believed it. How do you do it?" He smiled, patted Garret's shoulder and sighed. "Lady," he said to Adrianna as seriously as he could, "what's he got that I haven't got?" He waved his hand to stop her in case she should attempt to answer the question, turned, and walked away.

Adrianna stayed her anger to ponder what he'd meant. Even Garret was dumbfounded as he watched him leave the cafeteria.

"That's a funny thing for a racing official to say," she said.

"Racing official? That's Noel Bauer, the society

columnist. He doesn't know a racehorse from a mountain goat. You sure made a great impression on him," he said, staring her into silence with his ice-cold eyes. "For Pete's sake! He must think you were propositioning me!"

"How could he get an outrageous idea like that if he didn't have good cause to believe such a thing in the first place?" If he wasn't a racing official, then she had no reason to believe that Garret was going behind her back to keep Sarazen. She had it all figured wrong. "Oh, Garret," she said, hiding her face in her hands. *How can I ever apologize?*

"The game is over," he said, searching his jacket pockets.

"Over? What do you mean?"

"This!" He handed her an envelope and watched her intently for her reaction. "Open it. It's a subpoena. For me. I've been subpoenaed to answer charges brought against me for race tampering."

"What? I don't understand."

"Race tampering. They think I knowingly entered Sarazen in that race and had him lose."

"But why?"

"To defraud the track. Devalue his true potential. Enter him in lower and lower classes and have him lose every race so his betting odds would go higher and higher—setting him up for that one big gambling payoff."

"But . . . that's cheating."

"Come on, little girl, wake up. The unscrupulous do it all the time. Pay off the jockey to run a lousy race. Tie up the horse in the middle of the pack and never get him free to break away. Whoever is behind it was waiting for Sarazen to be entered in that claiming race."

"Who? Why?"

"To claim him for practically nothing and then race him with his odds up to a hundred to one."

"But I . . . my uncle and I claimed Sarazen."

"I know," he growled.

"You don't think that I . . . ? That my uncle . . . ?"

"Don't I?"

Chapter Ten

She didn't remember leaving the cafeteria. She didn't remember driving out of the track, or how she managed to get lost. She pulled off the road twice to stop and dry her eyes, and both times she had to concentrate extremely hard to remember where it was she was going and why. When she finally regained her bearings, a thunderstorm forced her off the road, and again she found herself in the car waiting for everything to become still.

So it was just not meant to be. Some things are just as natural and inevitable as a rainstorm. A time to cleanse, to wash away the dust of dreams and begin again. She let the seat back and watched the canvas top vibrate under the pounding rain.

He must have suspected her as an accomplice from the very first moment. Why else would he crash Alex's party but to gain her confidence and discover the truth about how Sarazen had been stolen away from him? Alex didn't want Sarazen. He'd tried to talk her out of claiming the horse. She knew she could convince Garret of that, convince him that he had made a mistake and should look elsewhere for his crooks. She had even withdrawn her claim and had torn up the check right in front of him and thrown it at him. All those tiny pieces catching in his hair, those wonderful black curls . . . .

And there would be no problem whatsoever convincing him that she loved him more than anyone else in the world. That would be so easy. Way too easy. She pictured herself joining in on the fun he must have had with all those plans. Plan A: pick the flower and put it in her hair; plan B: take her to the secret spot by the water and tell her she was the only one who had ever seen it; plan C: let her see the soft, vulnerable underside of the horse trainer consoling his injured horse before he destroys it. All of it had been a ploy played on a woman stupid enough to believe every word of it, every beautiful moment of it. Everything he did must have been a conscious effort to find some proof of her conspiracy to steal his horse. Oh, Garret!

He could keep Sarazen. He'd stop at nothing, he'd proven that—even making her fall in love with him—to get his horse back. Sarazen had to be very important to him to make him do such a thing. Adrianna hoped she never lived to learn how anything could be more important than love.

She had no idea how long she sat there, how long the thundershower lasted. The sun broke through for a moment and colored the droplets in the air into a violet rainbow that haloed the sky with promise and hope. Was nature mocking her? Or was that, too, just an illusion, like everything else?

She found her way back to the estate and parked

the sports car in the garage. She was the only one who had ever driven it, except for Garret the other night. The other night? A dream already claiming rights to her memory as one of the happiest moments of her life. She dried the car off with an old towel the chauffeur used and covered it with the tarpaulin Alex had bought to keep the dust off it and have it looking like new for her when she came to New York for a visit. As she zippered the cover shut, she knew in her heart that she would never drive that car again. It would be a long, long time before she would visit this estate again. Maybe never. Alex would do well to sell the car, or put it up on blocks so the tires wouldn't go bad and then store it for ten years. It would be a classic. Brand-new. Hardly any mileage.

She left a note for the chauffeur, telling him to suggest the idea to Alex. In any case, she would never drive it again, and it was now up to Alex to do with it as he pleased. If he insisted that she keep it, she'd protest that such a car in the rural wine-country of upper New York State would be a headache to own, an unnecessary burden that she and her father could ill afford.

The money she had saved to buy Sarazen would now pay for the new winepress her father would need when his first harvest came in. And if he refused to accept the money, she'd buy the press herself and have it delivered. *I will be investing in my own future,* she thought. *I have given up horses.* It was a silly girl's dream, a momentary infatuation. Almost a tragic mistake.

Marcie didn't hear her come in, at least she didn't call out from the kitchen. She peeked into Alex's study. He wasn't there. The limo had been missing from the garage. Off again. Gallivanting his adorable, charming self into the hearts of all who were lucky enough to know him. Was there anyone on earth having more fun than he? Anyone with a heart as big as his?

She sat at his desk and called the airport. There was one flight to Albany with just a two-hour wait for the shuttle plane that would bring her within an hour's drive of the farm. She could call her father when she arrived, wake him up to come pick her up and bring her back home. She dialed the number and let it ring twenty times. He was most likely out working his vineyards. She'd surprise him. Take a cab from the airport and just be there in the kitchen when he woke up the following morning.

She found a piece of stationery in the desk, took the pen from the holder and wrote Alex a note:

Dear irascible, cantankerous, pesty, impossible, most wonderful uncle in the entire world,

Where are you? If there is anyone on earth who needs to be married, it's you. When are you going to settle down? I'm going home now. This horse business wasn't such a good idea after all.

I don't know when I'll be back to see you. Maybe you can drop in on us sometime. I know you and Dad always argue, but that's because you insist on being so generous.

I love you and I always will.

Your niece,
Adrianna

She put the pen back in the holder and leaned the note up against it.

The kitchen was a mess of bundles and boxes. All the food Marcie had ordered yesterday must have arrived. She was busy putting it away. "There you are. Your uncle has been calling all day for you."

"Where is he? I want to say good-bye."

"Good-bye? Oh, child," she said, wiping her hands on her apron and walking over to her. "Your uncle told me everything. He's down at the hearing right now. He was subpoenaed this morning. Didn't have a chance to eat his breakfast and he was gone again. He called just a while ago to see if you were here. He left a number."

From the wall phone in the kitchen she dialed the number. It was the racing commissioner's office. Alex Trent was in conference, and he would have to be paged.

"Page him, please. I'll hold," Adrianna said. And to Marcie, "I never thought they would subpoena him. But of course they would. He made the claim. Oh, Marcie, what a mess this whole thing has turned out to be. Poor Alex. I just can't bear the thought that I brought all this down on his head. He wanted no part of the horse. I talked him into claiming him for me."

"Adrianna?"

"Uncle? Is that you? I'm sorry for all of this. I . . ."

"Sorry? What for?" he said. His voice was alive and vibrant, just the way it always was. "A lot of nonsense has been cleared up this afternoon. At the very least, it's safe to assume that Sarazen is the horse you always believed him to be. You've got a winner here, and by God, no one is going to take him from you. Not while I'm still alive."

"Uncle . . . it's too late for all of that now. I don't want Sarazen any longer. Please, for me, pull back the claim and let Garret . . . let Worthington Stables have their horse back."

"What's the matter with you? Have you gone daft? The evidence so far . . ."

"Uncle, please! I'm leaving. I'm going back home. Where I belong. This breeding business was a stupid idea from the very start."

"It's not a stupid idea. Not now it isn't. Forget what I said about everything."

"What are you doing down there? Answering charges of . . . of race tampering? When all you ever did was lend me your signature to claim a horse you advised me not to claim? I won't have it. I won't have you going through an inquisition. It's not fair."

"What inquisition? This is all part of the game. My reputation carries a lot of weight around here."

"It's too late, Uncle Alex. Please believe me, I want nothing more to do with Sarazen. I just can't live with the idea that I got you into this mess. Pull back the claim. Please. I have a flight out of Kennedy Airport in a couple of hours, and . . ."

"Baby?"

"What?"

"Don't run away."

"I'm not . . . running away." A tear escaped her without warning so quickly, she hardly knew she was crying. She cleared her throat and struggled to keep her voice unaffected and calm. "I'm going back where I belong. Good-bye, Uncle."

"Put Marcie on the phone."

"Marcie, he wants to talk to you." Adrianna wiped her eyes and ran up to her room to pack.

Sarazen was the most magnificent animal she had ever seen. But too much of him, all of him, was tied to Garret. How was it possible to look at that horse and not think of his trainer, how he could just whistle for him to come and how that black stallion would nudge his forehead into Garret's chest? Sarazen was his, all right. Morally, ethically, lovingly his. *Why, Garret? Why didn't you just announce your campaign to get him back? I would have understood.*

It started raining again, a heavy spring rain that beat the earth evenly and incessantly like sustained applause, a wonderful noise that softened the inside of a room and made one talk in a whisper.

She was nearly finished packing when Marcie tiptoed in with a tray. "Some tea? Let me warn you. It's an old-fashioned recipe, spiked with booze."

"Oh, Marcie, you know I don't drink much."

"Neither do I. But a little taste on a rainy night can't hurt. For the road, child." She placed the tray on the nightstand and poured two cups full from a fat porcelain Chinese pot. "This will take the chill off your bones," she said, handing Adrianna a hand-painted Chinese teacup. She took the matching cup for herself and sat on the bed. "God love you, child, but I sure hope you're doing the right thing."

"You too? I thought you had a dim view of horses? I should think my leaving all of that . . . nonsense . . . behind would have pleased you." Adrianna sat next to her and sipped the tea. It was delicious. If there was any whiskey in it, she couldn't taste it.

"I wasn't talking about horses," Marcie said, breaking eye contact with her.

"Oh?"

"Yes, oh."

"Let's leave it as it is, Marcie. Better not say anything more. I've made up my mind and that's that."

"I'll say one thing, and one thing only, child." She placed her hand on Adrianna's knee and looked her squarely in the eye. "When I caught you two rolling on the grass, didn't you see how much he loved you? I could see it all the way from the kitchen door. Didn't you see it?"

Adrianna didn't answer. She'd seen it . . . but it wasn't true. None of it was true. She would have said something, but a part of her told her that this woman was a romantic at heart, looking for love and finding it even when it wasn't there. Adrianna said nothing, just put her arms around Marcie's shoulders and kissed her on the cheek.

Marcie clicked her teacup against Adrianna's and smiled wistfully. "Drink up," she sighed. "What time is your plane?"

"I'll have to leave within the hour to be on the safe side. I'd better call a cab."

"I will," Marcie said, pouring Adrianna another cupful. "Have your tea and get dressed." She arose and carried the tray towards the door. "Wear something pretty. Let your hair down," she said, standing in the doorway. "Let me remember you as the beautiful young woman you truly are."

"Do you think Alex will be back soon? I forgot to ask him. I would like to see him to say good-bye."

"Who knows with that man? I don't think there's anything he would rather do than to embroil himself in a good fight," Marcie said, sweeping out of the room.

Adrianna put her brown slacks on the bed next to the jonquil-colored blouse with the lacy front. The outfit, with her tweed sports jacket, would be the most comfortable for traveling. It wasn't that long a trip in distance, but it was turning out to be the most fateful she would ever take. Going back to recoup, and soon—she hoped, soon—to begin again. The vineyard would never seem the same to her again.

Perhaps she would never really go home again. But in time, she would have a future again, something to aim for and accomplish, something to celebrate.

After she'd showered and dressed, she stood by the window to brush out her hair. It was too dark to see the lawn of the flower garden; her reflection got in the way. The sadness had ravaged her eyes, leaving them vacant and without hope. She would feel better after a good night's sleep, she told herself. In her own bed, in her own house.

She carried her luggage down the stairs and had to sit on the steps to regain her strength. She hadn't realized how tired she was. Exhausted. If she could only close her eyes for a moment, or just lie down to wait for the cab.

"Are you all right, child?" Marcie said, shaking her shoulder. "We already loaded your luggage in the cab. It's time to go."

"Already? I must have dozed off."

Marcie helped her to her feet and gave her a hearty hug. "Take good care of yourself," she said, her eyes welling up with tears.

"I will. You too. I'll call you when I . . . need someone to talk to."

"I'd like that, child. I'd like that a lot."

Marcie walked her out to the cab, ordering the driver to be extra careful. It had stopped raining but the roads were still wet. They kissed each other good-bye, and Adrianna watched her waving in the driveway until the cab turned out on the road.

"Miss Adams?" the cabbie said. "Are you okay?"

It was Junior. The rider she had met that morning.

"Junior? Is that you?"

"Yes, ma'am. My second job."

"What a wonderful coincidence. I let Sarazen go. I hope someday you get the chance to ride him." She caught herself yawning and quickly covered her mouth. "It's so nice to see you again. Would you mind terribly if I nap awhile?" She slouched in the large seat and felt the muscles in her neck begin to relax. "Wake me when we're there. I wish you all the luck in the world . . . " was the last thing she remembered saying as she felt her entire body melt away from her, disappearing into the night without the slightest resistance. The tea had been stronger than she'd realized. It was her last thought before she fell totally and completely into oblivion.

So warm, so wonderfully caught in the moments before awakening to relish the simple joy of each muscle luxuriating in comfort. She had dreamt of him carrying her in his arms, kissing her tenderly on the lips. How many nights would that ghost invade her emotions, seduce and impassion them only to leave her awake and empty?

She turned over in the bed. The heavy quilt counterpane pressed against her body, massaging her as she moved beneath it. The air in the room was cool against her cheek, and that made her all the more aware of how warm and cozy she was under the covers. What a wonderful bed, she thought. Why hadn't she noticed it before? How soft . . . a bed?

She opened her eyes and, without daring to move, studied the flowery print of the paper covering the wall facing her. A cheerful yellow, with daffodils that reflected the sunlight coming in from the window. Her heart started to race, and she cautiously sat up and looked around the beautiful little bedroom. A dormer window was open, and the sheer curtains in front of it breathed softly in the light.

Where am I? The cab? Junior? She'd only closed her eyes for a moment. She had her nightgown on.

Her luggage was standing in the corner; a suitcase was unstrapped and lay open on the floor. Her brown slacks, blouse and tweed jacket were on a hanger hooked to the back of the door. The door was slightly ajar, and from behind it she heard voices from very far away. The ceiling was slanted drastically, and the dormer window cut out of it told her she was on the top floor of a house, in part of an attic that had been converted into this lovely room.

Somehow the voices reassured her. The small nightstand next to the bed had an antique Tiffany lamp. Around its base was an intricately woven lace doily. The knobs on the doors to the room, the closet, and the door leading to a small bathroom were white porcelain on shiny brass door plates. A chest of drawers with white porcelain handles stood opposite the foot of the bed. On the wall behind it was an oblong mirror framed in wood that was decoratively carved. All those details combined with one another to make up the charming ambience. It was difficult not to feel safe in a room like this, she thought.

She tiptoed across the room and peeked out the door. Down the hall was a stairway that descended sharply to the left. Rising up from it were the voices, a little louder but barely intelligible. She looked out the window and into the sun high up off the ocean. East. On the coast. Close to a beach that stretched as far as she could see in either direction.

The bathroom had a pedestal sink with fat porcelain faucet handles shaped like bloated crosses. The bathtub was an old-fashioned fixture on ball-and-claw feet, with exposed brass plumbing.

How on earth did I ever get here, wherever here is. Kidnapped? Held for ransom? Her uncle's fortune? No. Those thoughts came too late to have any validity. Her door was unlocked. And kidnappers didn't dress their victims for bed and hang up their clothes.

She rummaged through her luggage for her jeans and work boots. She put on her blue denim blouse and a red bandanna around her neck. She was not the least bit frightened, though it was all utterly unexplainable. To wake up in a strange room not knowing how, or why, or who . . . The tea! Marcie's tea! How quickly she'd grown tired after drinking it! Alex! "Put Marcie back on the phone" was the last thing he said to her. *Put Marcie back on the phone. That . . . incorrigible . . .*

As she slowly walked down the stairs, the voices below grew increasingly louder. At least three of them, she thought as she looked about her on the landing.

The doors on either side of the hall were solid oak, framed with thick oak moldings. The hall floor had wooden tiles with a long throw-rug running down the center. The light entered from octagonal windows on each end. The glass was clear and etched with a floral design that complemented the late nineteenth-century decor. This staircase was twice as wide as the other one. It curved down into the center of the house, into a foyer behind an oak-and-glass front door. The voices were coming from the left.

She stepped into the dining room and into the heart of the nineteenth century. The table was small and made of cherry wood, accommodating six high-backed antique chairs. Above a fireplace and mantle was a portrait of a beautiful woman standing at the foot of a circular staircase. An antique highboy with a marble top graced the other wall. She let her hand skim the cool stone as she walked past it and stood behind the sliding glass door that led into the kitchen.

The voices were coming from there, along with the clinking of china and flatwear and the smell of bacon and fresh coffee.

The first voice she recognized was Garret's. She surmised that she was at his house in the Hamptons. Junior must have driven her there last night. He worked for Garret. That dream she had of him carrying her in his arms, kissing her lips . . . He'd carried her into bed! And undressed her! Her temper started to boil as her face reddened, but she stayed herself when she recognized Alex's voice. Alex? At least now she knew she was safe, she thought as she gathered herself before she stepped out from behind the door.

No, wait. This must have been his idea. If I was drugged, it was under his orders. Put Marcie on the phone! Her temper got hold of her, and she stepped out into the doorway.

They were seated in a breakfast nook surrounded by windows that opened out onto the ocean and the morning sea-breeze. The kitchen was large and modern, with a butcher-block central stove and brass pots and utensils hanging from the ceiling on chrome hooks. An elderly woman was standing before them, pouring them coffee. Garret saw her first, and the rest stopped talking and turned. The woman was beautiful. Adrianna recognized her as the one in the portrait over the mantle. She wore her hair the same way, only now the color had changed from black to silver. Her smile was disarming, and she hurried over to Adrianna and extended her hand.

"Adrianna. Welcome. I've heard so much about you, I feel I've known you all my life. I'm Maureen. Garret's grandmother."

"How do you do," she said, shaking her hand.

"You have me at a disadvantage. How on earth did I get here?"

"Those two," she said, nodding her head at the men in the alcove. "It was an awful thing to do, and I gave them hell for it. Come, have some coffee. How do you feel? Any side effects?"

"Then I was drugged?"

"Your uncle is a very determined man. If I wasn't convinced that he loves you so much, I'd be out of my mind with anger. Whoever heard of such a thing? When Garret carried you in here last night, I didn't know what to think. Alex convinced me that you were fine and a good night's sleep was all that you needed. You do look okay to me. My, you are pretty."

The woman linked her arm through Adrianna's and walked her to the alcove. Garret arose. He was still dressed in the same shirt and tie he'd worn in the cafeteria. He needed a shave, and he looked as if he'd been up all night. Alex remained sitting and just smiled sheepishly up at her. He, too, was rumpled and in need of repair.

"I don't want to hear it," Alex said, raising his hand to stop her before she could speak. "I know how you must feel. And I'm sorry. But I had to do something. I just couldn't stand by and watch you throw your life away."

Garret fixed on her the excited, vibrant stare of a man breathless at the sight of her. His lips moved softly as if he were whispering something private, something he hoped she would understand.

"May I talk with you a moment?" he said, taking her hand and leading her out the back door onto a small porch. When he closed the door behind him, Adrianna turned her back and watched the surf pound the deserted beach. Gigantic waves broke high above the beach and crashed into the sand with violent abandon. Strange that such power could be virtually silent, just an echo on the sea breeze that wafted through her hair.

Standing behind her, he placed his large, powerful hands on her shoulders and let them slide down her arms. He hunched over her till his hands reached her hips and his lips were pressed against her ear. "Forgive me. I made a mistake." His hot breath sent chills cascading down her spine, and she leaned back and into him, enveloping herself inside his arms. "I love you. I loved you from the first moment I saw you," he whispered, biting her earlobe. "Believe me, I'm never, ever going to let you get out of my life. Ever! I've kidnapped you once, I'll kidnap you again. And again, if necessary. However long it takes to convince you."

She turned around in his arms and looked up into the worried sky of his eyes, sinking her fingers into those luscious black curls.

The breeze blew her long blond hair to either side of his face, forming a pocket, a shield in which she could be alone with him, this man who silenced the roaring ocean and called the wind to witness their union.

"Maybe it won't take that long to convince me," she said, looking in his eyes and finding in them the passion she felt in her body. "Then again, maybe I'll just enjoy the convincing so much, you'll just have to keep on convincing me. Am I making any sense?"

"I love you so much!"

Chapter Eleven

"Honestly, Adrianna, I couldn't blame him, not that I wasn't angry at the young whelp for brandishing his accusations. I used to be the same way," Alex said, taking a sip of his coffee and shaking his head at the memory. "He's passionate and he knows what he wants. But a bit rash, a little too quick to exact his piece of flesh when a little patience would serve him a lot better."

Maureen was sitting next to Alex in the booth, listening to his every word and nodding at the appropriate time, when he hit upon a long-understood truth she knew about her grandson.

"Isn't that the truth?" she said, shooting a glance Garret's way.

"But his instincts were right, after all," Alex said, "and that's the important thing. If a horseman doesn't have instincts, he has nothing. Your suspicions were correct, Garret. All that we need to decide upon is the most appropriate, and propitious, moment to make it all pay off. For all of us."

"Uncle?" Adrianna and Garret were sitting across from them, holding hands under the table. "You're leaping ahead. Where am I?" she said, turning to Garret, "and how did I get here?"

"You're at my house in the Hamptons," Garret said. "This is my grandmother. Grandmother, this is Adrianna."

"Thank you, dear boy, I gathered all of that," Maureen replied. "What Adrianna wants to know is how you two conspired to get her here and why. Am I right, dear?"

"How and why," she said, giving Garret's hand a squeeze. "I should be furious at you both."

Alex took another sip of coffee and smiled at her. "Allow me to tell my side of it first, if you don't mind, Garret," he said.

"By all means, Mr. Trent," Garret said, nodding his consent.

"Cut out that Mr. Trent stuff. It's Alex to you. Get used to it. It appears that we'll be seeing a lot of each other from now on. That is, if we can keep my niece from running away again."

"Uncle, will you please . . . ?"

"Okay, okay. I got this summons to appear before the racing commission, along with Garret and Old Man Worthington himself. Someone tipped off the authorities that Sarazen was being held back, made to lose his races to increase his betting odds. Garret accused me, a likely candidate inasmuch as I claimed the horse. I accused Worthington because he knew that no one in his right mind would claim a horse who had lost every one of his races as badly as Sarazen did. He wouldn't be taking much of a chance entering Sarazen in the claiming race. It was a good cover-up.

Worthington pleaded innocent and accused Garret. Garret, after all, had the opportunity, the expertise, and the means to run the scam and get away with it.

"In the heat of the examination, the commissioner suspended Garret and Sarazen from racing until the matter could be cleared up. Worthington couldn't have cared less. All he wanted was for his name to be cleared so that his entire stable wouldn't be suspended. I hit the roof. I wanted the horse for you, and I insisted on my legitimate claim to him. Garret got to his feet and demanded that criminal charges be filed against him so that he might have his day in court to prove his innocence. Why don't you pick it up from there?"

"I couldn't say anything right there, in front of everyone," Garret said. "It was Lydia and Floyd Hess who were behind it all, but I wanted to be absolutely sure before accusing them. I wanted to tell Worthington of my suspicions in private, and I wanted to confront Lydia and Floyd and wring the truth from them."

"And just then," Alex jumped in, "who do you suppose came into the commissioner's office to drive her father home?"

"Lydia?"

Garret nodded. "It couldn't have been better timed. Worthington introduced her to the commissioner, who offhandedly asked her if she knew me well enough to vouch for my character. She was still angry about that night at Arpeggio's, and she started on a rampage about how I banned her from the stables and how she was going to talk to her father to have me fired as an incompetent trainer."

"The commissioner picked up on that," Alex said, "and probed her for more information. Before she realized it, she was being cross-examined by me, her father and the commissioner. Garret was just sitting there looking as inconspicuous as the Sphinx. It was Worthington himself who asked her who gave the okay to enter Sarazen in the claiming race."

"At that point, she cracked," Garret said.

"It was very embarrassing, to say the least," Alex said.

"She admitted to getting Floyd Hess to bribe the jockey to run Sarazen badly," Garret said. "'Make him lose and lose and lose,' she said, to get even with me. She couldn't stand the idea that I had shunned her. In spite, she set out to discredit me. Money never entered into it as far as she was concerned. Floyd Hess was setting that up for himself. It must have been him who tipped off the commissioner when he saw that Sarazen was legally claimed. There's a subpoena out for him right now. And Lydia will have to face a charge of conspiring to race tampering."

"While all of that was going on," Alex said, "you called. I couldn't explain anything to you over the phone. All I knew was I had to do something to keep you from running away."

"Marcie?"

"I told her to put a sleeping pill in the tea," Alex said, arching his eyebrows and daring to smile. "What else was I going to do? Garret sent over one of his riders, who works as a cabbie, to drive you here. That's it. The whole story."

"And you carried me upstairs to the bedroom?" Adrianna asked Garret.

"Yes. And put you to bed."

"You undressed me?"

"He would have, believe me, my dear," Maureen said, "if I wasn't there to stop him. I managed to tuck you into bed."

"I told you you'd be safe here, didn't I?" Garret said.

"And safe you will be," Maureen said, "for as long as you wish to stay."

Garret turned to his grandmother. "Someday you'll realize that there's such a thing as being too safe," he teased.

"Not where you're concerned. Adrianna is much too pretty to allow the wolf in you any chance at all," she laughed.

"See?" Garret said, putting his arm around Adrianna's shoulder. "Nothing to fear for as long as you decide to stay. Do stay."

"What about Sarazen?"

"I've got him," Alex said, "or should I say, we have him. He's in the barn out back."

"He's here? Why?"

"Why? My dear," Alex said, hunching forward, "you've got to get him ready to race."

"To race? What race? Why didn't you leave him at the track?"

"I'm not taking any more chances with him," Garret said. "I have no way of knowing how many people were involved in this fraud. I want him here, where I know he'll be safe."

"I . . . I don't understand," Adrianna said, placing her elbows on the table and pushing her hands through her hair. "Both of you seem to have everything worked out to your mutual satisfaction. All the loose ends tied up. It must have been very easy with me in a coma and quietly out of the way. What race are you talking about? What about my plans—taking my horse and trailering him back up to my farm? Does anybody remember that? Or maybe I didn't make myself very clear. I appreciate all you've both done to get Sarazen. I know how fond you are of the animal, Garret. Keeping him here is just your way of not letting him go. Maybe . . . you should have him after all. Pay Alex the claiming price and keep him."

"I couldn't, even if I wanted to," he said. "Who'll believe I was innocent of setting him up for a low claiming price if I wind up owning him? No, he's yours. Or Alex's."

"Legally, maybe. But . . . he's your horse, and you know it."

"He's my horse," Alex said, "for the moment. And I'll do with him what I will. He stays here. Garret and I decided . . . we discussed the possibilities of entering him in the Nassau Invitational. I know I can swing that with the track, convince them he's worthy of such a test. If you and Garret train him, get him ready."

"Garret and I? He has a stable full of horses to train. And I don't know the first thing . . ."

"Not anymore, I don't," Garret said. "I quit Worthington Stables. For the first time in my life, I'm unemployed. What do you say? Do we have a working arrangement or not?"

"And I'm supposed to stay here, in this house, to . . ."

"To be close to Sarazen. What else?" He smiled.

"Nothing else," Maureen added.

"Adrianna, look," Alex said, reaching for her hands. "It's the only way. What chance would you have breeding Sarazen? His reputation is that of a loser. No one in his right mind would buy a horse sired by him. He has to prove himself. Win a big race in a big way. Garret believes the horse can do it. So do I. So do you. You've got to do it or you have nothing, less than nothing. The purse will be over two hundred thousand dollars."

"And what's in it for you, Garret?" she asked.

"Nothing. Just to see Sarazen earn the respect he's been cheated out of. That's all I want."

"And you, Uncle?"

"Little girl, all I want is what's best for you."

"At one time, you thought it best for me to sail away with Jerald Montgomery."

Alex eyed her sideways and tried not to react. He admired her, and it showed in the way he looked at her.

"I'm not perfect. I make mistakes."

"Maybe racing Sarazen is another mistake?" she speculated.

"Not for me," Alex replied. "I've got nothing to lose. Garret's putting up the entry fee."

"Garret? Why? How much?"

"Ten thousand dollars," Garret said. Maureen lowered her eyes and slowly shook her head.

"What if he loses?" Adrianna asked him.

"He won't."

"What if he does?"

"Then we're both out. You, six thousand, and me, ten."

"I can't let you do that," Adrianna said, watching Maureen still silently shaking her head.

"It's hopeless, my dear," Maureen said. "When he makes up his mind, it's hopeless to try and change it."

"If Sarazen wins, and he will," Garret said, "you give me back my ten thousand, plus my fee for training him and the cost of the feed. Deal?"

"And I go back to the farm with a winner and two hundred thousand dollars?"

"You do whatever you want," Garret said. "I need him to race, to prove to the world he's a champion. Give him that chance. Deal?"

"I'll have to think about it," she said, studying his eyes and finding the sincerity and determination she always felt was so characteristic of him.

"Good," he said, "think about it. Now let me out of here. I'm so tired, I could hibernate for a month. Alex, if you get Sarazen into that race, he'll be ready to run. I'll guarantee it. Grandma, don't put Adrianna to work too soon. I need her fresh and energetic. We start training tomorrow at four-thirty A.M. Junior says you have the makings of a first-class jock," he said to Adrianna as he stood up. "We'll see. There's an empty field a mile from here that's in pretty good shape for running. We'll inspect it tomorrow. Mark off five or six furlongs and concentrate on bringing home a winner. I'm going to bed."

"If I were to consider racing him, how much time would we have?" Adrianna asked.

"Two weeks."

Whatever doubts she'd had about racing Sarazen were now completely satisfied. Garret and Alex were right; reputation was of paramount importance, the crucial ingredient in her breeding plans. And Garret needed her horse to win, if only to prove to himself that what he had always suspected about Sarazen was true. But still, she couldn't allow him to risk his money, especially now, when he was out of a job. She would think of some way to raise the entry fee, even borrow it from Alex if she couldn't get a loan. Raising the money would be the least of her problems. Convincing Garret that it was her responsibility as the owner to take the risks would be another matter. *Two weeks is a long time. A long time to . . . discuss the possibilities, agree upon the definitions and strike the most equitable solution.*

Garret leaned over and kissed her softly on the lips. It was a strange feeling for Adrianna to have witnesses to this show of affection. Strange, but somehow reassuring, as if Garret and she had come a long way together. He loved her. She could see it in his eyes and feel it in her stomach. That thought was enough to tighten her chest and steal her breath away. Living in the same house for nearly the next two weeks was going to challenge their love and define the commitment she hoped with all her heart he was ready to give her. She sensed all of that in the instant he pulled away from her and offered his hand to Alex. She wondered if he knew it, too.

He kissed his grandmother on the forehead and gave her a tender hug. "Stop worrying, Gran. You know how I hate it when you worry. You always told me when I was a boy to go after whatever it was I set my heart to. Didn't you?"

She nodded at him and smiled so wistfully, it brought tears to Adrianna's eyes.

"Well," he said, "I'm doing just that."

"That's what has me so worried," Maureen said. "Such a beautiful horse and so gorgeous a young lady—that's more than enough to test any man's heart."

Garret winked at Adrianna and kissed his grandmother on the forehead again. "She's always worried about my heart. As if there is only so much love in it and I have to be real careful how I mete it out, and to whom."

"That's not it at all, and you know it," Maureen said, playfully shoving him away. "It's just that you two seem to have something . . . wonderful. I don't want anything to happen to it."

"Me too, Gran," he said, fixing Adrianna with his brilliant blue eyes. "Me too."

When Garret left, Alex decided he, too, was in desperate need of sleep. Adrianna and Maureen walked him outside to his limo. His chauffeur must have just arrived; the engine was still running.

"So," he said to Maureen as they approached the car, "do we have a date?"

"Sounds exciting," she said. "I haven't been to a Broadway play in twenty years. I can't wait."

"I'll send the car to pick you up at two o'clock. You should be at the mansion by three for cocktails. We'll leave by four for an early dinner before the show."

"You certainly don't waste a moment to make a date, do you, Uncle?" Adrianna said.

"A moment? Child, I've been up with Maureen all night long. I feel I've known her all my life."

"True enough." Maureen smiled. "We're old friends now. Well, Alex, I better get some sleep, too, or I'll never make it. It's almost eight o'clock already."

"Eight in the morning? Is that all it is?" Adrianna said.

"I'm afraid I won't be much of a hostess for you today, my dear."

"You were the only one that got any sleep at all last night," Alex said.

"I gathered that," Adrianna said. "Well, Maureen, if you're brave enough to go out with my uncle, then I'm brave enough to be alone with your grandson."

The thought had never occurred to Maureen. Her eyes widened as she realized her promise to be a chaperone had already been broken.

"Maureen, believe me," Alex said, "Adrianna is old enough to take care of herself. Aren't you, my dear?"

"Of course I am," she said. "I think. Though those eyes of Garret's are hypnotizing," she teased.

"Then don't look at them," Alex said. "Maureen, the limo will be back at two. Till then, sweet dreams.

Adrianna . . ." He wanted to say something paternal, but he thought better of it. "Let me know if Garret needs anything, anything at all for Sarazen."

They watched the car pull out of the drive and disappear under the oak and elm trees lining both sides of the highway. About a mile away, Adrianna could see a small cluster of pitched roofs poking up through the trees in a picture-perfect setting. That had to be the center of town. Adrianna decided to walk there later for a visit. She wanted to know everything there was to know about the town. With both Maureen and Garret asleep, it would be the ideal time to explore it at her leisure.

Maureen took her arm and led her through the house and back into the kitchen. "I want you to consider this house yours," she said. "There's plenty to eat in the pantry. Please feel free to poke into everything. I'm so happy to have you here. I've waited for you for a long, long time, and now you're finally here."

"Waited for me? I don't understand."

"You're the very first girl Garret ever brought home. I guess he must have been waiting for you for a long time, too. What a sight when he walked in here with you asleep in his arms. This is your house for as long as you care to stay. I hope you stay forever." She kissed Adrianna on the cheek. "The barn is out back. If you want to take a drive into town, the keys to the car are hanging on the hall tree near the front door. I've got to get some rest. Tell me, is Alex really as wonderful as he seems?"

After Maureen went upstairs, Adrianna walked out to the barn, a solid old white structure with a weather vane on top of its gambrel roof. Sarazen was in a large stall, quiet as a thundercloud trapped in stillness.

She stroked his face and tried to sense if he knew

anything at all about what he was going to be asked to do, if he had the same urgency to succeed that always knotted Adrianna's stomach and made her grit her teeth. *Do you know? Do you feel the storm clouds gathering on the horizon? Two weeks, Sarazen. Just two weeks.* She slipped him a slice of apple she had taken from the kitchen.

She went back to the house and poured herself a cup of coffee. The kitchen was so peaceful and quiet, she could hear the ocean breeze whispering in the curtains. A walk into town might just be the thing to ease the tension and anxiety beginning to build inside her. She finished her coffee and climbed the stairs to her room to get her purse.

The door to the attic staircase was open. She peeked in and saw Garret stretched out on a bed, lying on his back with his hands crossed over his taut stomach muscles. He wore just the bottom half of a jogging suit. His powerful naked chest rose and fell slowly as he slept. The sight of him renewed her longing to be near him, and she entered the room just to touch his face and kiss him softly on the forehead. Ever so gently, she sat on the edge of the bed to watch him, to inhale the power and determination he exuded, to feel his strength and let it soothe her anxious heart.

He turned slowly towards her and put his arm across her lap. "Stay," he whispered. He didn't open his eyes, and she didn't know if he was awake or not. "Stay with me. Forever."

Chapter Twelve

Adrianna must have fallen asleep. When she heard the limo pull into the drive, she got up and looked out the window. Maureen was ready and waiting, dressed in a long evening gown and a mink stole. They would make a dashing couple. She wished she could see the two of them together, all dressed up and eager to paint the town.

Garret got up and came over to her. Together they watched Maureen get into the car.

"What are you doing in my room?" he whispered into her ear, wrapping his arms around her waist and holding her tightly.

"I just came in to look out the window." Would he believe that? "Your grandmother is so beautiful. She and Alex make a wonderful couple, don't you think?"

"We're alone. Just you and me. What a great opportunity for . . ."

"Garret—"

". . . for us to get to work. What did you think I was going to say?" he teased. "I'll show you the field I picked out to train on. We can stake out the curves and rope them off," he said, sliding his hands over her hips. "Just so the day won't be a total waste." He turned her towards the door and gave her a gentle shove.

A few minutes later they were loading the trunk of his car with long wooden stakes, balls of twine and all the old rags they could find in the barn.

"We'll strip these rags and tie them to the twine," he said. "Simulate a rail as best we can. If we work fast, we can get most of it marked out before it gets dark."

The field was a short distance away, about a hundred yards in from the highway. What Garret liked most about it was a small knoll in the center from which an observer would have a perfect view of the horse at all times. Half of the prospective track was a soft dirt road which they walked over very carefully, inspecting for potholes, ruts and large stones. Garret carried a shovel, which he used from time to time to dig out rocks and fill in any depressions he thought were dangerous. The other half of the track was perfectly flat, with nothing on it but small weeds and wild grass.

They walked that part just as carefully, inspecting it for rocks and gopher holes. All in all, it was in fairly good shape. It would serve their purposes for the time being.

"On the fourth night before the race, we bring Sarazen to your uncle's stalls at the track. Get him acclimated once again to the real thing. The next three days, we run him under race conditions, the whole mile and a half, as if it were the race itself. How does that sound to you?"

"It sounds like you know what you're doing," she said.

"I think I do."

"I know you do."

They staked out the curves and tied the strips of rag to the twine. The sun had already set when they walked to the top of the knoll to inspect their work.

"I'm going to ask Junior to run him each morning," Garret said.

"I can run him."

"No, you can't. Not the way he'll have to be paced, held back and let go at just the precise moments. You'll run him in the late afternoons to keep his conditioning up to form. We're not taking any chances with anything."

"Junior is going to come way out here each morning? That's a lot to ask of him, isn't it?"

"Maybe. I'm paying him what he'll earn at the track. He wanted to do it for nothing if I'd let him ride Sarazen in the race. He gets his license this week sometime."

"I told him that if I ever raced Sarazen, I would let him ride him," Adrianna said.

"We may want someone with more experience."

"Think you'll get a top-name jockey to ride a horse with Sarazen's reputation?"

"You think Junior can ride that well?"

"I don't know if he can or if he can't. All I know is he has a feeling for the horse and I can trust that. I know he'll give it everything he has and more. That's good enough for me."

He sat down on the knoll and pulled her down into his lap. "You're the owner. Whatever you say goes. If you feel that strongly about Junior, well, that's good enough for me."

"Of course, it goes without saying that I don't know what I'm doing," she said, putting her arms around his neck.

"Of course," he said, trying to kiss her.

She pulled back. "You don't have to agree with me!"

"I will if what you say is true. I'll let you know if I think you're in over your head," he said. "We don't have the luxury to waste time arguing about who's right and who's wrong. Decisions have to be made, right or wrong. I'm not going to allow anything to get in the way of the job that has to be done."

"You have it all worked out, don't you? Maybe I'll be in the way? We both agree that I don't know anything at all about anything. Maybe I should just go back to Alex's and wait to see how it all turns out? Would you like that?"

"I'll let you know. If you get to be a real liability, I'll drive you there myself." He rolled her over in the grass and tried to kiss her on the neck.

"Get off of me!" she screamed. "You . . . you . . . arrogant . . ."

He laughed as he jumped to his feet, and she leaped up to race after him. He let her catch him at the base of the hill, and he swung her around and around in his arms.

"I'm never going to let you go, no matter how big a liability you are," he laughed, holding her up by the waist at arm's length and slowly letting her down into his arms. "Never!"

The next nine days were the most arduous of Adrianna's life. At four-thirty every morning, she met with Garret and Junior in the kitchen and planned the morning workouts. Garret kept charts that coordinated Sarazen's timed sprints at various distances with precise amounts of feed and water, which he carefully adjusted each day at preset intervals. He and Junior decided how the horse would be run, how far and at what speed.

Each day Garret would move a marker, a red flag tied to a large stake, a set distance further away from a similar marker along the full reign and encourage Sarazen to run his hardest along that route. The second flag marked the finish line. The time it took Sarazen to cover the distance in between was carefully timed by Adrianna and Garret.

Junior's riding was severely tested and challenged. He had to bring Sarazen up to the first flag at precisely the right speed in order to maximize the stretch drive without overexpending the horse's energy.

"A controlled, elongated explosion," was how Garret put it. "Speed is one thing. To sustain that speed, endure the agony of lungs burning with exhaustion, reach the threshold of pain where there is nothing left to give, and then give more—that's a champion. All we are doing, and make no mistake about it, is conditioning Sarazen to be ready to give that immeasurable more. Whether he will or he won't, we'll never know until that moment in the race when Junior signals him that this is it. We can measure his power and rate his speed, but we can't measure his desire to win. That's the intangible that makes all the difference in the world."

Walking back from the field each day, Garret would question Junior about his technique, some flaw that only a careful observer with a trained eye could spot, and drill the rider in the points to be especially careful about. Timing, pacing, position. There was no room for mental mistakes, not with a field full of horses tunneling into a turn.

"This is child's play, Junior. You have to know at every second in the race where you are, how to correct and overcome a bad position, what mistakes you make that Sarazen can and cannot be expected to compensate for."

Each evening Adrianna rode Sarazen through a series of conditioning exercises, wind sprints that Garret observed and timed. These sprints weren't nearly as fast as when Junior was riding, but they weren't meant to be. There was no critical observation about form or technique. Only once did Garret make a comment about her riding, the same comment Junior had made—her rear was too high.

Their afternoons were free. After lunch, they would walk Sarazen down to the deserted beach and let him go romp in the surf. Whenever he got too far away, Garret would only have to whistle to bring him charging back. These idyllic hours were the only respite in their schedule, and Adrianna hungered for them more and more each day. It was their time to be alone, when the worries and anxieties of the race were lifted from them. After dinner and the evening workouts, they were both too tired for much conversation. Twice in the past week and a half, when Alex had come to visit Maureen and the four of them were lounging in the living room, Adrianna had fallen asleep and Garret had carried her to her room.

He would kiss her good night and she would wake up in his arms half-asleep, half-dreaming that he was going to stay with her. He wanted to desperately. The fire in his eyes always left her wondering, expectant, longing to share the ardor burning deep inside her. But his contract with Maureen, an understanding between them that transcended words, was inviolate. There was always tomorrow on the beach, when they could talk and hold each other for hours.

Their last afternoon together, they left Sarazen in the barn and strolled along the beach towards their favorite spot among the dunes, a hollow where the sun could warm their bodies and dry the surf from the legs of their jeans.

Tonight they would trailer Sarazen to Alex's stables at the track and Adrianna would return to the mansion. What reason was there to stay out here with Sarazen gone? Only one, the intangible that made all the difference in the world, the commitment from him that would allow her to give herself to him freely and fully forever. She knew everything about him, his family, how Maureen had raised him when his parents tragically died. And nothing was a surprise, in the sense that it all confirmed what she had felt to be true of him. Principled, honest, with a great deal of integrity and inner strength. Strange that she could never mention to him how she longed to hear the words that said she was the one woman, the one person he wanted to spend the rest of his life with.

"I gave Alex the purse money already," he said when they sat down on the blanket. "It had to be this way, so if you're going to go into a tirade, go ahead. But it's not going to change anything."

She knew he had given Alex the money, and she knew there was no use arguing about it. When he set his mind to do something, there was no stopping him. But when she set her mind, there was no stopping her, either.

"I know."

"You do? You're not mad?"

"What good would it do?" she asked.

"No good," he said, stroking her hair. "I know"—
his voice softened—"how irritating I can get,
and . . . I'm sorry, really I am. But I have to do this.
Go the limit. Put it all on the line."

"So do I."

"It's not enough to say you believe in something
and then let others take the risks for you. I can't do
that."

"I know," she said. "It all comes down to that
intangible you were talking about, doesn't it?"

"How do you mean?"

"That certain something you hope Sarazen has to
give when called upon to give it."

"Stride for stride, that horse is as good as or bet
ter than any other horse in that race. I know it. I
can prove it. But yes, it does come down to that
intangible. That's true of most things, don't you
think? You can figure something out, be ninety-nine
percent sure, but unless it happens, you never really
know."

"You never can be sure about anything unless you
take a chance," she said. She leaned against him and
outlined his lips with her fingertip.

"We are certainly doing that. Your life's savings
and mine."

"It's only money. That can be replaced. If we lose it
all, we still have . . . our families," she said.

"We still have each other," he said, searching her
eyes for a clue as to where this conversation was going
to lead.

"Do we?"

"No matter what happens," he said tentatively,
"we'll still be together."

"How can you be so sure?" she said, tracing his
eyebrows before letting her hand relish the curls

behind his head. "I have a father in upstate New York who is going to need all the help he can get. You have a grandmother who needs you to run things here."

"What are you saying?" he said, pulling her shoulders into his chest.

"I'm saying that . . . we have more at stake in this race than our life's savings."

He looked at her for a long moment, and she never felt as sure as she did at that moment that he was going to ask her to marry him. But he just kissed her softly on the lips as he held her tightly in his arms.

For practically the entire day, even when they were together in the cab of his pickup with Sarazen in the horse trailer behind, heading towards the track, he said nothing definite. The future of their relationship was in his hands. There was nothing else that she had to say.

"I want Junior to run Sarazen at night also," he said to her after Sarazen was safely locked in Alex's stables. Maybe that was his way of saying that there was no future for them, she thought. "We have just three more training days, and I need the nightly workouts to be run with as much precision as possible. It will give Junior that much more time to fine-tune himself to the horse. You understand?"

"Of course. I have all the faith in the world in your judgment. I could use the rest. No sense for me to be hanging around here, anyway. I'll only be in the way. Why don't we agree not to see each other until the day of the race? It'll give us both a chance to think things over about how . . . things will go after the race. If we win or if we lose."

He reached out for her, but she turned away. Alex was waiting to drive her back to the estate.

"Adrianna!" Garret called after her, but she didn't stop or turn. When she entered the limo, she gave him a small wave. He just stood there with his hands on his hips, watching her go.

Sorry, Garret, she said to herself as she watched him out of the rear windshield, *but this is the only way. I want you, but only if I can have you forever.*

For Adrianna, the next three days were a never-ending torture. She tried too hard to busy herself with distractions, anything that would consume her attention long enough to ease her anxiety over the fact that in one afternoon, in the space of one horse race, she would know the course her entire life was going to take. It no longer mattered to her if Sarazen won or lost. One way or the other, her life was going to change. What mattered was the race that ended with two hearts beating as one. What more was there to risk than that?

And that race was being run right now, in the emptiness of her heart. That race could only be won by losing, losing one's self to the heart of another. A test that demanded each go the limit, with everything on the line. Garret was willing to bet his life's savings on the outcome of a horse race. Was he willing to bet his life, lose his heart to her, forever?

The morning of the big day couldn't arrive soon enough for her. There were a hundred distractions that filled her mind, but nothing that could ease the tension and anxiety. She spent an hour on the phone with her father, telling him about Garret, about Sarazen, about how the outcome of this one race was going to change her life. Her father wished her luck and told her what she wanted him to tell her, what she always knew in her heart to be true but never tired of hearing from him.

"No matter what, I'm always here for you."

"Thanks, Dad. I'll call you later and let you know what happened. I love you."

When Maureen came into her room to visit, Adrianna was startled to see the older woman and almost asked her what she was doing there. Adrianna had forgotten that Alex had invited her to the races. They had been seeing a lot of each other since they met. Maureen sat down on the bed and smiled so warmly, Adrianna felt like hugging her.

"How do you feel, Adrianna? You look too nervous to even think," she said.

"I am nervous. Anxious, really. I want this day to be over. How's Garret?"

"Garret? I was going to ask you. Haven't you seen him?"

"Not since we drove Sarazen to the track."

"Nothing serious, I hope."

"I . . . don't know. He's had a lot on his mind these past weeks. The pressure is very intense. If this is what it means to race horses, I'm glad I decided to breed them instead."

"He loves you."

"I know. He told me."

"He loves you a lot."

How much is a lot, she wondered. Enough to want to spend the rest of his life with her? "I'm going to have to get dressed, Maureen. I want to be in the paddock area before the race."

"Of course. I'll be in the grandstand with Alex, rooting for you all the way."

"Rooting for Sarazen, you mean."

"Him, too."

The Nassau Invitational was the seventh race of the nine scheduled for that day. Alex and Maureen planned to arrive by the fifth or sixth, but Adrianna couldn't wait that long. The third race had just gone off when she drove into the stable area and parked under the trees. She glanced down the street toward Alex's stables. There was a lot of activity, but she saw no one whom she recognized.

It was a long walk to the paddock, the corral where the horses that were about to race were paraded for the fans. Garret would be there eventually, leading Sarazen by the bridle. Junior would be on top in his racing silks, sporting the Trent Stable colors, blue and white. She would wait there for them on the wooden bench that circled the large chestnut tree. She would buy a racing form, handicap the opposition, and wait, in the tightening grip of expectancy. Wait.

The horses for the fifth race were led into the paddock, and the fans grouped three-deep to get a closer look at them. There was a tension in the air around the horses about to be raced, an explosive quality that exuded from their gleaming, prancing bodies. It was invigorating, compelling, like a hush that envelops an audience about to witness something extraordinary.

A half hour later, the horses for the sixth race were led in for review. Again, people crowded as close to them as they could, within the very fist of tension that rippled the shining horseflesh and punched breath through the flared nostrils. When they were led out onto the track, Adrianna positioned herself next to the paddock rail. At last the horses for the seventh race were led in.

The lead horse drew most of the people to the paddock, and by the time the third one had entered, the crowd was again three-deep, crackling with electricity. Garret led Sarazen by the bridle, just as she'd imagined he would. Junior was radiant in his blue-and-whites, and Adrianna held her breath. She knew the crowd was stunned by Sarazen's beauty.

Garret wore a tweed sports jacket and light tan slacks. He was looking over the crowd, searching for her. When their eyes met, he led Sarazen over to her and reached for her hand. "This is it. Any last-minute instructions for our jockey?"

She stood on the middle rail of the fence and grabbed Junior's wrist.

"Yes, ma'am?"

"Just do what you know how to do. Let him go when he's ready to run, and just hang on the best you can."

"I'll bring him back a winner, don't you worry."

Garret winked at her; and as he led Sarazen away, he called back over his shoulder, "Meet me at the rail down by the finish line! We'll watch the race from there!"

"Okay!"

The moment of truth was now. She made her way through the crowd and out into the uproar of the grandstand as the sixth race came into the stretch drive. She looked up at the grandstand where she thought her uncle and Maureen would be seated. She didn't see them.

Garret arrived a few minutes after the sixth race had ended. Together they made their way up to the rail and watched as the horses for the seventh race walked slowly out onto the track.

"How does it look to you?" Adrianna said. Only

then did she realize that she had never bothered to look over the field and rate the other horses in the race.

"Good. Great, as a matter of fact," he said, eyeing her dress and smiling. She was wearing the same sundress she'd worn on their date to Arpeggio's.

"How's the competition?"

"There is no competition," he said, placing his hands on her shoulders. Were they talking about the same thing?

"You checked out all the other horses in the race?" she asked, not knowing what to make of his seemingly placid disposition.

"I've checked everything I need to check. I know now how it's going to turn out." He looked deeply into her eyes, a smile threatening to part his lips.

"You do?"

"I do," he said. He took her hand, and silently they watched the horses parade in front of the grandstand, turn, and then slowly trot out to the starting gate.

"Sarazen has the worst starting position possible," she said. "If Junior doesn't get him out of the chute and into that first turn in a decent position . . . What do you think?"

"I think I've never been happier in my life," he said. He held up his binoculars and surveyed the horses as they were being set into the gates.

"How can you be so . . . so cool? What if he loses?" she said, irritated that he could be so calm at such a moment as this.

"Because no matter what happens out there, it's not going to change a thing."

"Not change a thing? Our life's savings are in the hands of an inexperienced jockey riding a horse that has never won a race and starting from the worst position on the track!"

"Crazy, isn't it?" he laughed. He stood in front of her with his back to the track and again placed his hands on her shoulders. "It's only money." He nodded back at the track.

"Money? And a career, and a business, and a reputation . . ."

"There is something more important than all of that." The bell went off, and the crowd around them stiffened as they waited for the announcer to call the positions of the horses as they rounded the first turn.

"What could be more important than that?" She knew the answer, but did he?

"Us. You and me. Let's make a real wager on this race. If Sarazen loses, we get married as soon as the race is over."

The people around them were getting excited, and they stretched their necks to see the race. The grandstand was starting to stir, rumbling like an approaching thunderstorm. She heard Sarazen's name over the P.A. along with the name of another horse. She heard Sarazen's name again. He must be near the front or in the lead!

"And if he wins?" she said. She had to shout in order for him to hear her over the roar of the crowd.

"If he wins," he shouted back, "we'll have to wait until the ceremony in the winner's circle is over before we get married. What do you say?" He leaned forward and coaxed her with a kiss. "Do we have a deal?"

She flung her arms around his neck, and tears of joy streamed uncontrollably down her cheeks. "Yes! Yes! We have a deal! Oh, yes!"

They missed the finish, so enraptured were they in each other's arms. But it didn't matter which horse came in first, not now. Even if Sarazen did set a new track record and win by four lengths going away. What was that compared to the victory of two hearts embraced in each other's love?

WIN

a fabulous $50,000 diamond jewelry collection

ENTER

by filling out the coupon below and mailing it by September 30, 1985

Send entries to:

U.S.
Silhouette Diamond Sweepstakes
P.O. Box 779
Madison Square Station
New York, NY 10159

Canada
Silhouette Diamond Sweepstakes
Suite 191
238 Davenport Road
Toronto, Ontario M5R 1J6

SILHOUETTE DIAMOND SWEEPSTAKES ENTRY FORM

☐ Mrs. ☐ Miss ☐ Ms ☐ Mr.

NAME _____ (please print)

ADDRESS _____ APT. #

CITY _____

STATE/(PROV.) _____

ZIP/(POSTAL CODE) _____

RTD-A-1

RULES FOR SILHOUETTE DIAMOND SWEEPSTAKES

OFFICIAL RULES—NO PURCHASE NECESSARY

1. Silhouette Diamond Sweepstakes is open to Canadian (except Quebec) and United States residents 18 years or older at the time of entry. Employees and immediate families of the publishers of Silhouette, their affiliates, retailers, distributors, printers, agencies and RONALD SMILEY INC. are excluded.

2. To enter, print your name and address on the official entry form or on a 3" x 5" slip of paper. You may enter as often as you choose, but each envelope must contain only one entry. Mail entries first class in Canada to Silhouette Diamond Sweepstakes, Suite 191, 238 Davenport Road, Toronto, Ontario M5R 1J6. In the United States, mail to Silhouette Diamond Sweepstakes, P.O. Box 779, Madison Square Station, New York, NY 10159. Entries must be postmarked between February 1 and September 30, 1985. Silhouette is not responsible for lost, late or misdirected mail.

3. First Prize of diamond jewelry, consisting of a necklace, ring, bracelet and earrings will be awarded. Approximate retail value is $50,000 U.S./$62,500 Canadian. Second Prize of 100 Silhouette Home Reader Service Subscriptions will be awarded. Approximate retail value of each is $162.00 U.S./$180.00 Canadian. No substitution, duplication, cash redemption or transfer of prizes will be permitted. Odds of winning depend upon the number of valid entries received. One prize to a family or household. Income taxes, other taxes and insurance on First Prize are the sole responsibility of the winners.

4. Winners will be selected under the supervision of RONALD SMILEY INC., an independent judging organization whose decisions are final, by random drawings from valid entries postmarked by September 30, 1985, and received no later than October 7, 1985. Entry in this sweepstakes indicates your awareness of the Official Rules. Winners who are residents of Canada must answer correctly a time-related arithmetical skill-testing question to qualify. First Prize winner will be notified by certified mail and must submit an Affidavit of Compliance within 10 days of notification. Returned Affidavits or prizes that are refused or undeliverable will result in alternative names being randomly drawn. Winners may be asked for use of their name and photo at no additional compensation.

5. For a First Prize winner list, send a stamped self-addressed envelope postmarked by September 30, 1985. In Canada, mail to Silhouette Diamond Contest Winner, Suite 309, 238 Davenport Road, Toronto, Ontario M5R 1J6. In the United States, mail to Silhouette Diamond Contest Winner, P.O. Box 182, Bowling Green Station, New York, NY 10274. This offer will appear in Silhouette publications and at participating retailers. Offer void in Quebec and subject to all Federal, Provincial, State and Municipal laws and regulations and wherever prohibited or restricted by law.

SDR-A-1

*Fall in love again for the first time
every time you read a Silhouette Romance novel.*

If you enjoyed this book, and you're ready to be carried away by more tender romance...get 4 romance novels FREE when you become a Silhouette Romance home subscriber.

Act now and we'll send you four touching Silhouette Romance novels. They're our gift to introduce you to our convenient home subscription service. Every month, we'll send you six new Silhouette Romance books. Look them over for 15 days. If you keep them, pay just $11.70 for all six. Or return them at no charge.

We'll mail your books to you two full months *before they are available anywhere else.* Plus, with every shipment, you'll receive the Silhouette Books Newsletter absolutely free. *And Silhouette Romance is delivered free.*

Mail the coupon today to get your four free books—and more romance than you ever bargained for.

Silhouette Romance is a service mark and a registered trademark.

- - - - - **MAIL COUPON TODAY** - - - - -

Silhouette Romance®
120 Brighton Road, P.O. Box 5084, Clifton, N.J. 07015-5084

☐ Yes, please send me FREE and without obligation, 4 exciting Silhouette Romance novels. Unless you hear from me after I receive my 4 FREE books, please send me 6 new books to preview each month. I understand that you will bill me just $1.95 each for a total of $11.70—with no additional shipping, handling or other charges. **There is no minimum number of books that I must buy, and I can cancel anytime I wish.** The first 4 books are mine to keep, even if I never take a single additional book.

☐ Mrs. ☐ Miss ☐ Ms. ☐ Mr.   BRR3L5

Name	(please print)	
Address		Apt. No
City	State	Zip
( )		
Area Code Telephone Number		

Signature (If under 18, parent or guardian must sign.)

This offer limited to one per customer. Terms and prices subject to change. Your enrollment is subject to acceptance by Silhouette Books.

SRR-R-A

She fought for a bold future
until she could no longer
ignore the…

ECHO OF THUNDER

MAURA SEGER

Author of **Eye of the Storm**

ECHO OF THUNDER is the love story of James
Callahan and Alexis Brockton, who forge a union
that must withstand the pressures of their own
desires and the challenge of building a new television
empire.

Author Maura Seger's writing has been described by
Romantic Times as having a "superb blend of
historical perspective, exciting romance and a deep
and abiding passion for the human soul."

**Available at your favorite
retail outlet in SEPTEMBER.**

ECO-B-1

Silhouette Romance

COMING NEXT MONTH

NOTHING LOST—Laurie Paige
Donna Whitaker's pride held her together after Alex
Hofstedder left her waiting at the altar. Now he was back in
town, claiming to love her, and his devastating presence
threatened to crumble her resolve.

RELUCTANT BRIDE—Doris Lee
Vicky had been only sixteen when she first lost her heart to Jeff
Hudson. Now she was a woman, and Jeff wanted to marry
her...but for all the wrong reasons.

AN OBVIOUS VIRTUE—Arlene James
Gene Brannick was willing to love, but only on his terms.
Destry, with the help of her large, loving family, was
determined to teach him the art of give and take.

EYE OF THE WIND—Elizabeth Hunter
Caring for Bart Bennett's convalescing daughter seemed like a
good job for Jane Lister. Then she found herself caught
between her growing passion for her patient's father, and the
sudden reappearance of her mysterious mother.

MERMAID—Victoria Glenn
Diana Mueller was hauntingly familiar. Wasn't it her sultry
voice Chase had been hearing in his dreams? Diana held tight
to her secret, in spite of Chase's determined challenge.

WISH UPON A STAR—Cassandra Bishop
Jane Jones, professional image maker, had transformed
herself into a fashionable package. Astrophysicist Hank
Mosely had no use for facades. So why did he find himself
intrigued by the woman underneath the glitter?

AVAILABLE THIS MONTH